BEST PRACTICE

What Reviewers Say About
Carsen Taite's Work

Drawn

"This book held my attention from start to finish. I'm a huge Taite fan and I love it when she writes lesbian crime romance books. Because Taite knows so much about the law, it gives her books an authentic feel that I love. ...Ms. Taite builds the relationship between the main characters with a strong bond and excellent chemistry. Both characters are opposites in many ways but their attraction is undeniable and sizzling."—*LezReview Books.com*

Out of Practice

"Taite combines legal and relationship drama to create this realistic and deeply enjoyable lesbian romance. ...The reliably engaging Taite neatly balances romance and red-hot passion with a plausible legal story line, well-drawn characters, and pitch-perfect pacing that culminates in the requisite heartfelt happily-ever-after."
—*Publishers Weekly*

"*Out of Practice* is a perfect beach read because it's sexy and breezy. There's something effortless about Abby and Roxanne's relationship, even with its occasional challenges, and I loved that I never doubted that they were right for each other."—*Lesbian Review*

Leading the Witness

"…a very enjoyable lesbian crime investigation drama book with a romance on the side. 4.5 stars."—*LezReviewBooks.com*

"…this might be one of Taite's best books. The plotting is solid, the pacing is tight. …*Leading the Witness* is a thrill ride and it's well worth picking up."—*Lesbian Review*

Practice Makes Perfect

"Absolutely brilliant! …I was hooked reading this story. It was intense, thrilling in that way legal matters get to the nitty gritty and instil tension between parties, fast paced, and laced with angst. …Very slow burn romance, which not only excites me but makes me get so lost in the story."—*LESBIreviewed*

Pursuit of Happiness

"This was a quick, fun and sexy read. …It was enjoyable to read about a political landscape filled with out-and-proud LGBTQIA+ folks winning elections."—Katie Pierce, Librarian

"An out presidential candidate (Meredith Mitchell) who is not afraid to follow her heart during campaigning. That is truly utopia. A public defender (Stevie Palmer) who is leery about getting involved with the would-be president. The two women are very interesting characters. The author does an excellent job of keeping their jobs in focus while creating a wonderful romance around the campaign and intense media focus. …Taite has written a book that draws you in. It had us hooked from the first paragraph to the last."—*Best Lesfic Reviews*

Love's Verdict

"Carsen Taite excels at writing legal thrillers with lesbian main characters using her experience as a criminal defense attorney."
—*Lez Review Books*

Outside the Law

"[A] fabulous closing to the Lone Star Law Series. ...Tanner and Sydney's journey back to each other is sweet, sexy and sure to keep you entertained."—*Romantic Reader Blog*

"This is by far the best book of the series and Ms. Taite has saved the best for last. Each book features a romance and the main characters, Tanner Cohen and Sydney Braswell are well rounded, lovable and their chemistry is sizzling. ...The book found the perfect balance between romance and thriller with a surprising twist at the end. Very entertaining read. Overall, a very good end of this series. Recommended for both romance and thriller fans. 4.5 stars."
—*Lez Review Books*

A More Perfect Union

"[*A More Perfect Union*] is a fabulously written tightly woven political/military intrigue with a large helping of romance. I enjoyed every minute and was on the edge of my seat the whole time. This one is a great read! Carsen Taite never disappoints!"
—*Romantic Reader Blog*

"Readers looking for a mix of intrigue and romance set against a political backdrop will want to pick up Taite's latest novel."—*RT Book Review*

when you pick up one of her books you are getting your money's worth time and time again. Consistency with a great legal drama is all but guaranteed."—*Romantic Reader Blog*

Above the Law

"…readers who enjoyed the first installment will find this a worthy second act."—*Publishers Weekly*

Reasonable Doubt

"I liked everything. The story is perfectly paced and plotted, and the characters had me rooting for them. It has a damn good first kiss too."—*Lesbian Review*

Lay Down the Law

"This book is AMAZING!!! The setting, the scenery, the people, the plot, wow. …I loved Peyton's tough-on-the-outside, crime fighting, intensely protective of those who are hers, badass self." —*Prism Book Alliance*

"I've enjoyed all of Carsen Taite's previous novels and this one was no different. The main characters were well-developed and intriguing, the supporting characters came across as very 'real' and the storyline was really gripping. The twists and turns had me so hooked I finished the book in one sitting."—Melina Bickard, Librarian, Waterloo Library (London)

Courtship

"Taite (*Switchblade*) keeps the stakes high as two beautiful and brilliant women fueled by professional ambitions face daunting emotional choices. ...As backroom politics, secrets, betrayals, and threats race to be resolved without political damage to the president, the cat-and-mouse relationship game between Addison and Julia has the reader rooting for them. Taite prolongs the fever-pitch tension to the final pages. This pleasant read with intelligent heroines, snappy dialogue, and political suspense will satisfy Taite's devoted fans and new readers alike."
—*Publishers Weekly*

Switchblade

"I enjoyed the book and it was a fun read—mystery, action, humour, and a bit of romance. Who could ask for more? If you've read and enjoyed Taite's legal novels, you'll like this. If you've read and enjoyed the two other books in this series, this one will definitely satisfy your Luca fix and I highly recommend picking it up. Highly recommended."—*C-Spot Reviews*

Battle Axe

"This second book is satisfying, substantial, and slick. Plus, it has heart and love coupled with Luca's array of weapons and a bad-ass verbal repertoire. ...I cannot imagine anyone not having a great time riding shotgun through all of Luca's escapades. I recommend hopping on Luca's band wagon and having a blast."—*Rainbow Book Reviews*

Beyond Innocence

"As you would expect, sparks and legal writs fly. What I liked about this book were the shades of grey (no, not the smutty Shades of Grey)—both in the relationship as well as the cases."
—*C-spot Reviews*

Nothing but the Truth

"Taite has written an excellent courtroom drama with two interesting women leading the cast of characters. Taite herself is a practicing defense attorney, and her courtroom scenes are clearly based on real knowledge. This should be another winner for Taite."—*Lambda Literary*

It Should be a Crime—*Lammy Finalist*

"Taite breathes life into her characters with elemental finesse. …A great read, told in the vein of a good old detective-type novel filled with criminal elements, thugs, and mobsters that will entertain and amuse."—*Lambda Literary*

Visit us at www.boldstrokesbooks.com

By the Author

Truelesbianlove.com

It Should Be a Crime

Do Not Disturb

Nothing But the Truth

The Best Defense

Beyond Innocence

Rush

Courtship

Reasonable Doubt

Without Justice

Sidebar

A More Perfect Union

Love's Verdict

Pursuit of Happiness

Leading the Witness

Drawn

Double Jeopardy (novella in Still Not Over You)

The Luca Bennett Mystery Series:

Slingshot

Battle Axe

Switchblade

Bow and Arrow (novella in Girls with Guns)

Lone Star Law Series:

Lay Down the Law

Above the Law

Letter of the Law

Outside the Law

Legal Affairs Romances:

Practice Makes Perfect

Out of Practice

Best Practice

BEST PRACTICE

by
Carsen Taite

2020

ISBN 13: 978-1-63555-361-1

This Trade Paperback Original Is Published By
Bold Strokes Books, Inc.
P.O. Box 249
Valley Falls, NY 12185

First Edition: October 2020

Credits
Editor: Cindy Cresap
Production Design: Susan Ramundo
Cover Design By Jeanine Henning

Acknowledgments

I've had a blast writing about this group of close friends which is really no surprise considering how much I value the female friendships in my own life. From the WEGS who bicycled through the streets of London to the dirty martini/old-fashioned/ hey, are they serving flights over there posse (you know who you are), the friendships I've found in this wonderful world of writing keep me sane and most important make me laugh. Special shout-outs to Georgia for the daily word count check-ins, Ruth for her magical blurb stylings, and Paula for reading every draft, listening to me drone on about plot points, and always being willing to don a snapback hat and act silly with me at home and abroad.

Thanks always to Rad and Sandy for making this publishing house a home. To my intrepid editor, Cindy Cresap—thanks for all the work you do behind the scenes to make my work shine. Jeanine, thank you for the beautiful set of covers for this series.

Thanks to my wife, Lainey, for always believing in my dreams even when they involve sacrificing our time together. That you are always available to brainstorm book ideas and plot points is a total bonus. I couldn't do this without you and I wouldn't want to.

And to my loyal readership, thank you, thank you, thank you. Every time you purchase one of my stories, you give me the gift of allowing me to make a living doing what I love. Thanks for taking this journey with me.

Dedication

To Lainey—you really are the best and I love you.

CHAPTER ONE

G race took a chance Judge Bonham wouldn't notice and glanced at her buzzing phone. The text from her best friend, Campbell, was both short and terrifying. *911 - Perry's in trouble.*

"Ms. Maldonado, what's your position on the motion?"

She shoved the phone into her briefcase and plastered on a smile. Luckily, she thrived on the ability to multitask. She pushed past Campbell's anxiety-inducing text and gambled she'd heard opposing counsel's arguments correctly. "We will agree to a continuance if the plaintiff will agree to mediation." She pulled out a sheet of paper. "I've prepared a list of names of possible mediators, all of whom are satisfactory to my client."

At the judge's nod, she handed the list to Leonard Greene, the attorney for Annie Fallon, the woman suing her client. Annie claimed the basket of the grocery store cart she'd been using had suddenly dropped to the ground while she'd been hanging on, causing her to suffer serious nerve injuries. Conveniently, the nerve injuries weren't the kind that would register on any objective testing and the offending grocery cart had either been tossed by store personnel or had been restocked with the rest of the carts, so no one could examine it to determine what had caused the alleged malfunction. The grocery store had settled with Annie for a nuisance sum, leaving Grace's client, Leighton Industries, the cart manufacturer, exposed to potentially large damages. Leighton had opted for trial, unwilling to consent to a big payout when there was absolutely no proof their product suffered from a manufacturing defect. Grace fully supported their decision, but if she could get the facts in front of a reputable mediator, maybe they could convince Annie that she didn't have a case since her attorney apparently lacked the skill to do so.

Leonard took the paper from her like it was a moldy slice of bread, scrunching his face into an exaggerated expression of distaste while he read the names she'd provided. Everyone on the list was a solid, qualified mediator, but she knew he'd hate them all because they would all see his client's case for what it was—a shameless money grab. He stood to address the judge. "Your Honor, these names are not acceptable to Ms. Fallon."

"I'm not sure how he knows that, Judge, since he didn't take the time to speak with her about them," Grace said. "If the plaintiff doesn't want to mediate the case, we're prepared to go to trial tomorrow." She delivered the declaration with confidence, but as Campbell's text hovered in the back of her mind, she prayed the judge wouldn't take her up on it. What was going on with Perry?

Judge Bonham shook his head at Leonard. "Mr. Greene, since this is not your first request for a continuance, I'm inclined to grant Ms. Maldonado's request. Ms. Fallon, do you understand if you don't agree to mediate the case, we'll be going to trial tomorrow? You're not required to come to an agreement in mediation, but you may decide you want to settle. Would you like a minute to confer with your attorney in private?"

Everyone stared at Annie who shifted in her seat, a grimace on her face. Grace had no idea if Annie's pain was real. The medical reports couldn't confirm any objective injuries, but pain was weird like that. Even if it hadn't been caused by an errant grocery cart, Annie might have gotten so used to the idea that she was an injured party, she was experiencing real symptoms. If that was the case, Grace felt sorry for her, but not enough to recommend her client pay big sums of money they didn't owe. She was paid to win, and she wasn't going to cave.

Leonard finished his whispered conversation with his client and turned back to face the judge. "We'll agree to mediate, but we'd like to propose our own list of mediators."

"I had a feeling you would," Judge Bonham said. "I'm granting your request for a continuance contingent on an agreement for a date and name of a mediator by Friday." He scrawled his signature on the order and handed it to his clerk before disappearing through the door behind the bench.

Grace didn't waste any time replying to Campbell's text. *Details, please.*

Stuck on phone. Get Abby and meet me at the office.

"Are you ready to pick someone reasonable?" Leonard stood behind her holding out a yellow legal pad with a handwritten list of names. "We'll agree to anyone on this list."

Grace stared at him for a split second before grabbing the pad. She tore off the sheet with the names and started walking out of the courtroom. Over her shoulder, she tossed out, "I'll get back to you tomorrow."

The minute she was in her car, she sent a text to Abby. *Group meeting. Conference room. Stat.*

Be right there.

Grace smiled at Abby's swift reply. She loved that she could count on her friends to drop whatever they were doing whenever one of them needed the superpower that came from marshaling their resources. A little over a year ago, she and her law school pals, Campbell and Abby, ditched their careers in big law to form their very own boutique law firm. Starting from scratch had been hard work, but it was also very rewarding, and a year out, they'd managed to build a nice book of business with the added bonus of being their own bosses. She instructed her car phone to call the office.

"Clark, Keane, and Maldonado, how may I assist you?" Graham, the firm's office manager, answered, his tone a balance of pleasant and professional.

"Graham, I'm headed back to the office for a meeting with Campbell and Abby. Put us on do not disturb for the next hour.

Also, I'm sending you a list of potential mediators for the Leighton case. Please locate an online bio for each of these names along with any other pertinent info you can find and get it to me by the end of the day."

"Yes, Grace. I shall commence the search posthaste upon receipt of the document you are transmitting."

Grace smiled at his strange formality of their office manager and rattled off a few more things she needed. She stopped at the light ahead and took a quick photo of the paper she'd taken from Leonard and texted it to Graham who was serving as the jack-of-all-trades at the firm. They'd been meaning to hire a full-time paralegal for a while, but they'd been too busy to buckle down on the search. As the managing partner of the firm, the duty fell to her, and she made a mental note to resume looking.

With business firmly squared away, she spent the rest of the drive wondering what could be wrong with Perry, Campbell's little sister. She shook her head. She knew Perry wasn't a little girl anymore—she'd recently graduated from law school, passed the bar, and was working overseas for a civil rights NGO, but the only image Grace could conjure up was that of a gangly young girl, spying on them when they were up late talking and trying to sneak a swig of the bottle of wine they'd swiped from Campbell and Perry's parents' liquor cabinet. It had been years since she'd seen Perry, and she had no clue what kind of trouble could have happened to cause Campbell to summon them all to meet.

She spotted Abby pulling in as she parked her SUV, and stood nearby, waiting before going inside. Campbell's Audi was already in the lot.

"What's the nine-one-one?" Abby called out as she approached. She pointed at Campbell's car. "I thought she and Wynne were at Leaderboard's offices all day today for trial prep."

"Good point. It's something to do with Perry, but I don't know what," Grace said, leading the way into the office. As they cleared the door, Graham leapt to his feet and motioned toward the conference room with a flourish.

"Campbell has requested the pleasure of your company for an urgent matter. She is waiting for you in there."

"Thanks, Graham. Hold all of our calls." Grace pushed through the door to the conference room. Campbell was on her cell and held up a finger to signal she'd be a minute.

"I understand," Campbell said to whoever was on the other end of the phone line, "but it's still not acceptable. She needs to get home as soon as possible, and I want to know what I need to do to make that happen. Call me when you have some answers." She disconnected the call and turned to face them. "Short version—Perry's NGO got booted out of Crimea last night without warning. They didn't have a chance to pack, and apparently, she and the other two lawyers she's been working with had to sneak out of town in the back of a truck. I have no idea how, but they made it to the UK and Perry doesn't have her passport or any of her visa papers so she's stuck there for now. Right now, she's staying with a contact of her boss in London." She pointed at the phone. "I called this guy I used to work with at Hart and Dunn. He did an internship at the state department and was always bragging that he had an inside track."

"She should go to the embassy," Grace said. "They can help her get a new passport. Your contact at Hart might be good, but I've got a pal who actually works for the state department and guess where he's stationed?"

"Really? I've got her birth certificate and a copy of her passport. I could overnight them to her in London, but..." Campbell's excitement faded.

"What is it?" Abby asked.

"I want her to come home. This is the second time she's been caught in a dangerous situation, but I know her. If I send her what she needs, she'll be back in some hot spot within twenty-four hours."

Campbell tapped the marble tabletop with her pen in a steady beat that Grace recognized as her stress mode. "Let me guess. You already talked to her about it and she shot you down."

"I barely got the words out before she started listing all the reasons she needs to get back to work," Campbell said. "I don't get it. I mean it's not like they're going to be able to go back to Crimea anytime soon, but she's talking about returning to Afghanistan now, and I just can't even. The minute I send her what she needs to get her new passport, I lose any leverage I have."

"What about asking Justin to talk to her?" Abby asked, referring to Campbell and Perry's older brother.

"He's at an off the grid retreat for work. I'm sure I could muscle someone into getting a message to him, but it's too late. She'll know we're tag-teaming her, and she's not going to respond any better to him than me."

"You're probably right about that," Grace said, remembering how Perry had rebelled against their older brother's attempt to fulfill the dad role after their parents died.

"I'd fly over there myself if I didn't have this damn trial starting in the morning. Judge Danzinger wouldn't grant a continuance if we showed up with the measles."

Campbell started the tapping thing again and Grace reached over and gently placed her hand on Campbell's to stop the drumbeat, while her brain started whirring toward a solution. "You sure you have all the paperwork Perry needs to get her passport?"

"Yes."

"Then give it to me. I'll take it to her and make the case for her to come home." Campbell started to protest, but Grace cut her off. "You're starting trial, and Perry is more likely to react to a friendly face than a phone call. My trial got continued, and since I'd cleared my schedule for the rest of the week, I've got the time. Besides, I can work on the plane." She stood to signal the matter was settled. "I'm going home to pack."

Campbell sighed. "I have to admit I'm relieved. I'll get Graham to book you a flight with an open return for you and Perry. First class, my treat." She held up a hand when Grace started to protest. "Don't argue with me."

It was Grace's turn to sigh. Campbell was trust fund wealthy, but she'd never gotten used to her easy generosity, evidence of which was scattered around the office, from the expensive, hand-carved marble conference room table to the fancy espresso machine in the kitchen. Grace usually drew the line at personal largess, preferring to pay her own way, but she supposed she could accept her generosity seeing as how she was doing Campbell a favor. "Okay, fine."

Campbell shook her hand to seal the deal. "And promise me you'll do something fun. You're the only one of us who hasn't taken a real vacation yet. It's London, baby—live it up!"

Grace laughed. She'd never be as carefree as Campbell, but maybe she could make this into a mini-vacay of sorts. She'd never been to London or anywhere outside of the US beyond a quick trip over the border with her parents to go shopping when she was young. She wasn't going to go wild, but perhaps she could find time to have a little bit of an adventure.

The voice was faint at first but grew louder as it became more persistent. Perry put a hand over her ear and rolled over in bed, hoping whoever it was would go away so she could get back to the hazy, but delicious dream about the hot blond lifeguard.

"Perry, wake up."

Ugh. She looked up to find her boss, Tom Dorsey, looming over her. As her eyes adjusted to the light, she could see his hair poking out in a dozen different directions, and he glanced around furtively, clearly agitated. She rubbed her face, trying desperately to wake up, but everything was fuzzy. She could've sworn she'd been sound asleep in her room, not dozing at her desk, but why would Tom be in her bedroom, and why did he look so frantic? "What's going on?"

"Get dressed," he whispered, his tone urgent. "We have to go. Right now."

His words still didn't make sense, but other details started to fall into focus. She could see through the slats of the window blinds that it was still dark outside. She looked over at the other bed in the room for Linda, the other lawyer who worked with her at Lawyers for Change, but it was empty. "What's going on?" she asked again, but before Tom answered, Linda appeared in the doorway of the bathroom, fully dressed.

"It's all yours, P," Linda said. "Tom, give us a sec?"

Tom glanced between them, "Yeah, okay. But make it fast. They'll be here any minute." He stepped out of the room and shut the door.

"What's going on?" Perry asked as she swung her legs out of bed.

"Our NGO permit has been revoked and we've got to be out of the country by dawn or we'll be arrested."

"Wait, what?" Perry shook her head. "They can't do that." The local Crimean government had been making noise about tossing them out for the past couple of weeks, but they'd written off the threats as propaganda and pressed on in their work with local counsel for Andre Numeroff, the journalist who had published a series of hard-hitting pieces decrying the injustices wrought by Russia's annexation of the country.

Linda pointed at her clothes hanging over the back of one of the two chairs in the room. "Talk and dress at the same time. You want to be the one who explains why we're still here to the police when they show up?"

Perry stood and picked up her jeans, shoving her legs into them at breakneck speed. She pulled a light sweater over her head and went to work lacing up her Docs. "What are we supposed to do?"

Linda shrugged. "We'll figure it out once we get somewhere safe. Tom's got a contact who's going to help us out of here."

"When are we coming back?" Perry asked, her mind firing in a dozen different directions, but still focused on the reason they were in Crimea in the first place. "Andre is counting on us."

"You can't defend rogue journalists if you're in jail with them. Seriously, P, step it up, we gotta get out of here." A loud knock on the door punctuated Linda's assessment.

"On it," Perry said, looking around the room for the rest of her belongings. She tried to ignore Tom's insistent voice while she scooped up her stuff and shoved it into the same worn duffel bag she'd used on her last two assignments with Lawyers for Change. Since she'd started working with the NGO, she'd become an expert at packing everything she owned into a small bundle she could carry over one arm. She'd gathered her clothes and iPad and was looking for her wallet, when Tom burst into the room.

"They're here. We have to go now." He pointed to the window where tiny pinpricks of light were starting to peek through from the rising sun. "Does that open?"

Perry was still trying to process his words, but Linda dove toward the window and wrestled it open. Tom boosted her up, and when Linda disappeared from view, Tom motioned to her. "Come on," he hissed.

"I need my wallet." Perry reopened the drawers on the only other piece of furniture in the room. "I swear I put it here yesterday when I got back from the jail."

Tom slammed his hand on the windowsill. "Now, Perry. Leave it." Loud voices sounded from the far side of the office and Tom pointed toward the door. "They will arrest us."

Shit. He was right. She'd always known there was a possibility of being arrested, but had never considered it might really happen. She slung her bag toward him and placed a hand on the windowsill. "Ready to roll."

Tom tossed her bag out the window and lifted her to the ledge. She jumped the few feet down to where Linda was waiting and then looked back up to watch Tom follow. A few seconds later, they were running as fast as they could away from the building where the three of them had worked and lived for the past month. Perry gasped for air. She wasn't out of shape, but she'd seen the local jail and the idea of being trapped on the other side of the bars for any length of time had her shaken up.

Tom dashed ahead and led them into a store, slowing his pace to a brisk walk once they crossed the threshold, which she and Linda matched. In the back of the store, he exchanged a few words with a man stocking shelves, and Perry was certain she witnessed Tom slip the guy a fistful of rubles. After the exchange, Tom led them out the rear door where a truck was waiting.

"Come on," Tom said, opening the rear door of the truck. A tall, imposing woman with her face half covered by a scarf was waiting on the other side. She held out her hand and helped them each climb into the back of the vehicle. When they were all inside, she pointed to the bed of the truck and mimed pulling to Tom. He pried back the cutout to reveal a small crawl space, probably enough to hold two average-sized people. The idea of the three of them holing up in there sent Perry's head spinning, and when Tom gestured for her to climb in, she shook her head. "I'm good."

"You'll be good once you get in there." He scowled. "It's not a request. We don't have time to argue."

"We won't all fit."

"You two will," he said, motioning to her and Linda. Linda grabbed her arm and led her toward the space.

"We got this," Linda told her, but Perry felt like the only thing she was getting was hives. She had two fears: small planes and small places. Otherwise, she faced life ready to kick ass and do whatever it took to right wrongs. Hell, if she could stand up to the Russian government and Crimean prosecutors, she could curl up in a hole for however long it took for them to get to safety. She stepped into the space, lay down, and tucked up as tight as she could without passing out. A moment later, Linda joined her in the big spoon position, and it was slightly comforting to feel the press of a familiar person. Tom leaned in and whispered, "Not a word. Marta will get you out of here. Don't come out until she says it's okay."

He leaned back and started to put the cutout back in place, but Perry reached up and grabbed the plywood to stop him. "What about you?" she asked.

"I've got a different ride—chopper, but there's only room for one. I'd switch with you—"

"No, I'm good." Perry shuddered at the offer of a ride in a helicopter.

"Fair enough. This way's better, I promise. I'll beat you there and have all the arrangements in place when you arrive."

Perry started to ask him where "there" was, but before she could get the words out, he faux saluted them and said, "See you at the airport. I've arranged for a charter."

Perry groaned. They'd be checking off her entire list of dreaded things. Well, at least they were having an experience unlike any her law school classmates would ever see. She could imagine some of the big shots in her class sitting in a cushy law firm right now, making serious bank, but doing mindless work. Nope, none of that for her. Life was an adventure, and if you didn't take advantage of all it had to offer, you'd die full of regrets.

She repeated the silent mantra over and over while Tom fixed the board in place and the truck pulled away from the building she'd begun to think of as home. As the truck bounced over the bumpy streets, she leaned into Linda and let out her pent up breath while she played Tom's words back. All they had to do was make it to the airport and everything would be fine. Whatever happened, she was going to have a hell of a story to tell.

CHAPTER TWO

Grace walked onto the plane and matched the number of her pod with her ticket, silently singing Campbell's praises as she settled into the large comfortable space. She'd flown plenty for work, but only on domestic flights and, as an associate, she'd always been relegated to coach, arriving at her destination tired and disheveled. She spent a moment playing with the seat adjustment, and after determining she'd be able to recline all the way into a horizontal sleeping position, she examined the bag of goodies tucked in the large side pocket. A full-sized blanket, not the thin scratchy kind airlines usually offered, a sleep mask, pajamas, and travel-sized toiletries.

"May I get you something to drink?"

Grace looked up from her plundering into the kind eyes of the male flight attendant. "I'd love a Manhattan, but I'll settle for a bourbon neat."

He grinned. "There will be no settling. I've got you covered. Is Bulleit Rye okay? It's my fav."

"It's perfect."

A few minutes later, he brought her drink and set it down with a few pieces of shortbread on a china plate. "This is my favorite flavor combo—bourbon and cookies. It's just a little something to tide you over until dinner, which we'll be serving as soon as we reach altitude. I'm Paul. Let me know if you need anything." He zipped off and she sipped her drink, enjoying the warm rush of the whiskey. The shortbread was fabulous, and she made a note to pick up some of the genuine article to bring home if she had time while she was in the midst of Mission Bring Perry Back to Austin.

She hadn't seen Perry since she'd attended their law school graduation six years ago. She'd been an idealistic, outspoken college student, hell-bent on saving the world from things like capitalism and big business. Apparently, her passions had only grown stronger since instead of the usual law firm internships, she'd opted to hook up with nonprofits focused on saving the world. Campbell had talked to Grace about her worries Perry would never move back to Austin and settle down, which Grace was certain stemmed from her wanting to keep what was left of her family close. She'd assured Campbell that Perry would eventually get the wanderlust out of her system, but she hadn't spent much time with her in so long, she wasn't entirely certain that was true.

"Don't you love first class?"

The silky voice tore Grace from her thoughts, and she looked across the aisle at the breathtaking blonde seated in the pod to her left. "I'm learning to," she said, raising her glass. "I certainly didn't expect to get an excellent Manhattan on board."

"Word. Although, I'm a margarita girl myself." She tipped her glass in Grace's direction. "These aren't quite as good as the ones I make, but they're pretty darn tasty for airline fare."

Grace raised her glass in a virtual toast and took another sip just as the captain came over the loudspeaker to announce details about their flight. The blonde settled back in her seat and she followed suit, thinking that so far everything about this trip was more vacation-like than rescue scenario. She'd compiled a list of things to accomplish during the flight—make a list of bullet points for why Perry should come home, email her friend at the state department to get details on how to expedite the passport, prepare notes for the opening statement of her upcoming trial—but now that she was settled into her very own cubby on a transatlantic jet with a perfect drink, a beautiful neighbor, and hours of nighttime ahead, she decided to relax and enjoy herself for a bit. She put on the soundproof headphones that came with the pod, pulled up a book on her iPad, tucked her feet under the blanket, and started a mystery she'd downloaded while waiting to board. The story was riveting, but it was no match for the cozy blanket and the white noise hum of the plane's engines, and before long the words started to swim on the page. After dozing past her place in the story twice, she shoved the tablet in the side pocket and gave in to the solace of a nap.

Grace had no idea how much time had passed when she woke to the sound of a cart bumping down the aisle. It took a few minutes for her eyes to adjust to the low light in the cabin, and a glance at her watch told her she'd been asleep for about an hour. She couldn't remember the last time she'd taken a nap, but considering how refreshed she felt, she should probably find a way to fit them into her schedule more often.

"Ms. Maldonado, are you ready for your dinner?" Paul asked as he pulled up next to her seat.

"I am," she said, realizing she was ravenous. Must've been the nap. "But I'd really like a moment to freshen up if that's okay."

"Of course. Take your time and I'll bring your meal when you're ready." He consulted a card in his hand. "I don't have a choice listed for you."

He rattled off a couple of gourmet sounding selections and she chose a braised short rib and asked for another Manhattan, giving in to the idea she wasn't likely to get much work done once the lights went out again.

Once he moved on to the next passenger, she slipped her shoes on, grabbed her purse, and made her way to the bathroom which, for better or worse, wasn't much different from the ones in coach. She stared at her reflection in the cloudy mirror and patted the puffy circles under her eyes. She'd been keeping lots of late nights preparing for the Leighton trial and helping put together financing for a few other cases the firm had recently taken on. She enjoyed her position as managing partner, but the lines on her face made it clear the work was taking its toll. Definitely need more naps. Resolution made, she finger brushed her hair back behind her ears, hearing her mother's voice echo in her head, "Don't hide that pretty face." The thought made her smile. She'd meant to call or text her parents before she left, since it seemed like you should tell your next of kin when you were leaving the country, but she hadn't managed to find a free moment. Probably for the best. They had tried many times to get her to travel with them and she'd always begged off for work. She could hear her father, the US senator, saying, "It's about time you expanded your horizons to take in other cultures," although she seriously doubted he was talking about jolly ole Britain for the first stop on her cultural exchange.

After dinner, the effects of a second drink hit and she drifted off to sleep, not bothering to fight the urge this time, figuring it would be better to be well rested when she arrived in London. When she woke again, it was still dark in the cabin. She checked her email, and found a message from Graham, with information for the hotel he'd booked for her, followed by a message from Campbell. Apparently, Perry was staying at a hostel outside of town, insistent on being independent. Grace figured Perry's desire to be her own person was going to be the biggest obstacle to convincing her to come home to Austin. She pulled a notebook and pen from her bag and jotted down a list of reasons to support her argument: security, family, familiarity, friends. It was a good list, but she wasn't sure she'd found the tipping point—the one thing that would win Perry over to her side. She started doodling things she doubted Perry had access to in the war-torn countries she insisted on calling home. Kate's Donuts, Torchy's Tacos, bats flying out from the Congress Street Bridge. Seriously, there was no competition when it came to Austin. All she had to do was get Perry to realize what she was missing.

With less than an hour before the flight was scheduled to land, she abandoned the idea of more sleep and ducked into the restroom to brush her teeth and freshen up again. Instead of returning directly to her seat, she decided to wander around for a bit to work off her pent up energy before she was confined to her seat for the descent.

She wound up at the snack station near the galley and spotted the blonde from the seat across from hers rummaging through the tray of snacks.

"I think you're only allowed to take one of those," Grace said in a whisper, fixing her face into a stern expression.

"I'm a platinum member," Blonde deadpanned as she scooped up no less than four packs of cookies. "Special privileges." She held out her free hand. "Danika Larsen, nice to meet you."

Grace instinctively took her outstretched hand and studied Danika's face, trying to tell if she was kidding or a cookie thief. "Grace Maldonado. I'd say it's nice to meet you too, but you took the last of the cookies, so I'm withholding final judgment."

Danika grinned and handed her a packet. "If a packet of cookies is all that's standing between being shunned and getting to know you better, then by all means, have the cookies."

Grace accepted them and Danika's fingers brushed hers with deliberate slowness during the exchange. It had been a long time, but she was certain Danika was flirting with her and it felt nice. "Thank you." She lingered, wanting to continue their contact, but not great at making small talk. Campbell and Abby were better at that. She was the behind-the-scenes, no-nonsense, get it done partner in the firm, but the plane was about to land and she would probably never see Danika again, so why not give a bit of flirting a go?

"Are you traveling for business or pleasure?" she asked.

Danika wiped a cookie crumb from her lip in an adorable move. "A little of both. You?"

"Same. What do you do?"

"Finance. Venture capital, acquisitions and mergers, that sort of thing." Danika rolled her eyes. "Go ahead and nod off now. Most women do."

"I doubt most women appreciate the beauty of math." Ugh, had she really just said that? Super dork in the house. She scrambled to come up with a decent exit line when she caught sight of Danika's big grin. "What?"

"That might be the nicest thing anyone's ever said to me."

Could it be she'd connected with a fellow dork? Danika was a striking beauty and a math nerd? Seemed too good to be true.

"What do you do?" Danika asked.

"I'm a lawyer." Grace watched for one of the two usual reactions. People were usually either impressed and curious or cautious and cagey.

"Really? What kind of law?"

"Our firm handles a variety of cases, but primarily corporate litigation." Encouraged by what appeared to be sincere interest, she added, "We represent Leaderboard," referring to the social media app that had just moved into the top spot in the market. Normally, she wouldn't divulge the identity of a client, but Leaderboard was listed on their website as a representative client and their CEO, Braxton Meadows, liked to brag that he'd hired an all-female law firm to handle their litigation.

"I bet you have lots of stories you can't tell."

Grace smiled, pleased to meet someone who actually got it. "I can't even tell you if I have stories."

Danika dangled a packet of cookies in front of her. "Not even for more of these?"

"I don't think it's fair that we've barely met and you already know one of my major weaknesses." Grace settled into the flirting, not her usual style, but she was actually having fun. "How long will you be in London?" She wrote the question off to small talk, but a small part of her acknowledged she had an underlying reason for wanting to know.

"It's open-ended at this point. Depends on how efficient my work is, but likely the rest of the week. I have a short list of tourist things I'd like to do if time permits. You?"

"Also not sure. Based on my research, the matter I'm handling shouldn't take more than a few days."

"Will that leave any time for catching the sights?"

Grace considered her ultimate goal, returning home with Perry in tow. Not exactly conducive to sightseeing. "Regrettably not."

"That's too bad. I had a vision of us strolling through the markets and stopping to taste gin along the way."

Grace started to laugh at the image of them guzzling gin and stumbling past vendor stalls, but she could tell by the earnest expression on Danika's face, the invite was sincere. Sensing their flirting was about to go off the rails, she managed a forced smile. "I'm more of a bourbon gal."

"Hence the Manhattan."

Pleased Danika remembered her drink, she returned the gesture. "And here I thought tequila was your liquor of choice."

"Oh, it is, but one of my favorite things to do is immerse in the local culture." She held up one of the packets she'd swiped from the snack station. "Gin and biscuits. Such a sacrifice."

The speaker crackled on and the captain's voice boomed from overhead, telling everyone to return to their seats and cautioning the flight attendants to prepare for landing. Grace had mixed feelings about the interruption, both enjoying her conversation with Danika and skittish about the flirtation with a complete stranger. She wasn't normally impulsive, but Danika's warm smile made her want to be. A little bit.

"I guess that's it for now," Danika said, pressing the last pack of shortbread into her hand. "If I don't see you at baggage claim, I hope you have a successful trip and get everything you came here for." She leaned in and whispered. "I'll be thinking about you when I'm sipping the gin."

Danika disappeared down the aisle, back to her pod. Grace stayed where she was for a moment, kicking herself for not saying anything more, not getting a number at least. Campbell and Abby would've at least gotten her number when they'd been single. She looked down at the cookies in her hand and felt something stiff behind the crinkly cookie packet. She scanned the business card. Danika Larsen, VP Finance. Hmmm. Looked like one of them was willing to take the first step. If she could get Perry squared away, maybe she'd have time to take the second.

Chapter Three

I don't understand why I can't go with you," Perry said, pacing the tiny room in the hostel outside of London. They'd been here since leaving Crimea, and she was getting restless.

"Uh, passport?" Linda said as she closed her suitcase and slid it off the bed. "Tom's been called back to headquarters and his 'whisk us out of the country' magic is currently unavailable."

Perry sat down on the bed and pulled Linda onto it with her. They'd spent the last couple of days here waiting for Campbell to send her birth certificate so she could apply for an emergency passport from the US embassy. At Tom's suggestion, she'd lain low, but she was sick of staying inside and tired of not having the freedom to go where she wanted and when. Seriously, she was a lawyer working to help people less fortunate, not an immigration dodger. Damn bureaucracies.

When they'd arrived in London, Tom had tried to get the NGO to intercede to help her get a new passport, but they hadn't wanted to draw attention to the fact one of their own had broken several immigration laws smuggling them into the UK since several of their big donors were UK institutions. She'd reached out to her sister, Campbell, who, as expected, immediately launched into a top ten list of why she should return to the US permanently. Campbell had finally agreed to send her documents, but it could be several days before she received a delivery, and judging by the dodgy front desk people at the hostel, she wasn't entirely sure she'd ever get the package. Now Linda was being shipped out, and she wouldn't have the distraction of their London fling to keep her mind off her predicament.

"You sure you can't stay one more day?" Perry asked, hating her needy tone.

Linda put a hand on her cheek. "I wish. This has been fun and I'm going to miss this." Her hand dropped lower, and she traced Perry's side with a single finger sending spasms of orgasmic memory shuddering through Perry's body. "Apparently, whatever it is can't wait."

"Fine." It wasn't fine.

"Are you going to stay here?" Linda asked.

"Yes." She didn't want to, but the out-of-the-way hostel met the very definition of laying low since no one paid attention to her since she was one of many young travelers passing through. "I'll be thinking about you while I'm sitting here doing jack shit. Hopefully, I'll be able to get my passport by the end of the week and join you." It was a big hope since she didn't really know where she'd be assigned once she could travel again.

"That would be nice, but you do what you have to do."

"What's that supposed to mean?" Perry asked.

Linda shrugged. "Nothing. I heard you talking to your sister. Sounds like she misses you."

"I'm not sure missing me is an accurate assessment. She definitely likes to know exactly where I am and what I'm doing at all times. If she had her way, I'd be wearing a suit and sitting behind a desk twelve hours a day."

Linda stood, leaned in, and kissed her. "Whatever you say, P. Stay safe and I'll see you soon, I hope."

Perry watched her leave, and a strong sense of loneliness swept over her. She'd lived in close proximity to Linda and Tom for the past couple of months, and now she was all alone, without a passport, in a country where no one needed her services or cared enough about what she did to make an exception to let her get back to work. It was all her fault for not keeping her papers close at hand, but she couldn't help but think the universe was conspiring against her, especially after she'd spoken to Campbell.

"Are you sure this isn't a sign it's time to come home?"

Perry could hear Campbell's attempt to keep the big sister know-it-all tone out of her voice, but it lurked beneath the surface and put her on edge. "You try rushing out of your house in the middle of the night and being smuggled out of the country in the floorboard of a truck. Even you might forget to pack everything you need under those circumstances."

"Doesn't happen a whole lot here in Austin. You know what does happen? Fun things. The kind of things that don't get you thrown in a foreign prison or killed."

"Are you going to send my birth certificate or not?" Perry's mind churned through other possibilities for getting it from the States before the cash Tom had given her ran out. She could ask Campbell for an advance on her trust fund, but she didn't want to admit she needed anything more than help getting her passport.

Campbell sighed. "Yes, I'm sending it. I'll let you know where you can pick it up as soon as I've made the arrangements."

That had been yesterday. Perry knew she should give Campbell time, but she'd expected to hear back by now. Frustrated at her inability to control her own fate, she climbed back in bed and pulled the covers over her head. A nap was the perfect cure to most anything, and she was going to make the most of it.

She had no idea how long she'd been asleep when the buzz of her phone rousted her from slumber. She swiped at the phone and squinted at the text from Campbell.

Package at the Savoy Hotel. Front desk. Offer to come home is always open, but whatever you decide, let me know where you land. Love you, C

Perry shook her head. Campbell's persistence and optimism was undeniable, but she wasn't giving in to the offer. She glanced around the room and packed her things. She'd likely come back here tonight, but the hostel didn't have anywhere for her to store her stuff, and since what she'd been able to cram into her duffle bag was all she had, she'd prefer to keep it close.

The Savoy was in the Strand in central London, and when Perry entered the lobby, she instantly felt underdressed and out of place in the posh and vast art deco space. The people waiting in line at the front desk likely were all looking forward to their luxury stay and had no idea most of the world lived in abject poverty so severe they thought buildings like this were palaces accessible only to royalty. Knowing Campbell, she probably thought the documents would be safer here than sending them directly to the hostel, not thinking about how Perry might be treated by the staff who were used to wealthy, well-dressed patrons, not scruffy, nonprofit lawyers.

After a few minutes' wait, the man behind the front desk motioned for her to step forward. "Checking in?"

"Uh, no. Not even. I'm here to pick up a delivery. Perry Clark. It's probably an envelope. Sent from the States by Campbell Clark." She stopped talking and watched him bend down and check a mysterious drawer beneath the counter, finally producing a standard size envelope.

"I'm going to need to see some identification," he said, holding the envelope slightly out of reach.

"You've got to be kidding." Perry slumped at the realization neither she nor Campbell had considered the hotel wouldn't just fork over her important documents without some proof of who she was, even if the whole reason she needed the documents was to prove that very fact. She had two choices: she could either leave in a huff or use her lawyer superpowers to come up with a good argument to convince Front Desk Guy she was legit. Only one option would get her what she needed to get back to work.

"Here's the deal. The contents of the envelope you're holding are the key to not only my future, but the future of people who've been deprived of essential freedoms. Have you ever felt robbed of the chance to live a better life? One where you felt respected and free to be whoever you wanted without fear of repercussions that might be life-threatening?" She paused to see if she was making any headway. Front Desk Guy wore the unflappable expression made famous by the Brits, but she sensed by the twitch of a smile at the corner of his lips that he might still have a heart underneath.

"Sir, I suggest you give her the package. Otherwise she's going to keep talking until your ears fall off."

Perry swung around in the direction of the voice to see her sister's best friend, Grace, standing two feet away, looking even more drop-dead gorgeous than she had when Perry used to fill her high school notebooks with Odes to Grace on the daily. Seeing Grace here, in a London hotel lobby, was surreal and more than a little exciting.

"Grace, what are you doing here?" she asked as she pulled Grace into a fierce hug. "I thought you were in biz with Campbell in Austin. Did you go back to big law?"

"Hang on," Grace said, signaling to the guy at the front desk. "Sir, I believe there's a question you're supposed to ask the intended recipient of that envelope. Perhaps it's written on the back?"

They both watched while he flipped it over. "Oh," he said. He fixed Perry with a penetrating stare. "What is the name of your childhood pet?"

Perry laughed. They'd never had a pet, but she'd begged her parents for a dog, and said if they got it for her she'd name it after her favorite character in *The Outsiders*. "Ponyboy."

He consulted the note on the envelope. "Very well, right you are." He handed it to Perry, and she tore it open and shook out the contents, but instead of the documents she needed, the only thing inside was a small folder with a keycard emblazoned with the hotel logo. She shoved her hand deeper into the envelope but came up empty. "What the hell?"

Grace handed the guy some pound notes, and took her arm, guiding her away from the desk where a line had formed. "That's your room key. Campbell thought you might like to have a comfortable place to wait until your passport is ready. I hear you've had it pretty rough since getting booted out of Crimea."

Perry's brain started churning. How did Campbell obtain a keycard and send it all the way back to London? Oh, wait, she could've called the hotel to make the arrangements. But what was Grace doing here? "Wait, I'm confused. What are you doing here again?"

Grace didn't answer at first, but Perry could tell her brain was churning, and she had a feeling she knew why. "Oh, I get it. Campbell sent you."

"Not exactly."

Perry raised her eyebrows, urging her to explain.

"I volunteered," Grace said, effectively sidestepping the question. She handed her an envelope. "There's cash in there from Campbell and your documents are locked in the safe in my room. I have a contact at the state department who's going to personally handle the processing of your replacement passport."

Perry stood. "Great. Let's go see them now."

"He's not in today, but we have an appointment for tomorrow." Grace pointed at the key in her hand. "Why don't you stow your stuff in your room and I'll buy you lunch."

From the time she was a little kid, Perry had believed there was no finer, smarter, more desirable female on the planet than Grace Maldonado. She was certain some embarrassing doodle hearts with hers and Grace's initials in the middle existed in the storage trunk where she kept all her grade school memorabilia, and she'd spent many sleepless youthful nights dreaming about what life would be like if she only had the courage to declare her love to Grace so they could live happily ever after.

Two things kept her dreams from being fulfilled: Grace barely noticed her except in a big sister, pat you on the head and tell you to run along kind of way, and Grace was her sister's best friend, which meant if Perry had acted on her fantasies, Campbell would've told her she was being silly and effectively crushed the crush.

Now Grace was asking her out which meant she was at least getting Grace's attention, but it was still in that "you're the little kid and I'll take care of you" kind of way—not fantasy making material.

But she wasn't the same little kid who'd trailed around after her big sister with an unrelenting crush on big sis's bestie. She'd traveled the world. She'd seen things—horrible things— and worked hard to make a difference. Campbell and Grace had graduated from law school and joined forces with the big fat wallets of corporate law, donating to causes, but never seeing crises with their own eyes. She might have a lead on them in the living real experiences department, but no matter how accomplished she might be, Grace would never see her for anything other than the pesky kid who'd found a million excuses to interrupt her time with Campbell.

"Come on," Grace said. "It's lunch. Not a lot to think about unless you think I'm here to poison you." She pointed at the key in Perry's hand. "Go put your stuff away and meet me back here."

As if on cue, Perry's stomach rumbled. She'd gotten up too late for breakfast at the hostel, and all she'd eaten the night before was some of those crazy good chili puffs the bartender at the pub had rummaged from behind the bar. "Okay. I'll be down in a sec."

While she waited for the elevator, she watched Grace take a seat in the lounge. Grace pulled out her phone and started typing, likely answering a message from a demanding client. It wasn't like Perry begrudged the hard work Grace, Abby, and Campbell did back in Austin, but she didn't understand how they could do the same thing, day in and day out.

The room was at the end of the hall on the twelfth floor, and when Perry pushed open the door, she immediately thought she'd walked into someone else's luxurious suite by mistake. The front room had a large wet bar and seating area with two couches. She wandered her way farther in to find a large master suite with a four-poster king-sized bed, a massive wardrobe, and a desk suitable for a corporate CEO. The bathroom was bigger than two rooms at the hostel, and it was outfitted with cushy towels and fancy soaps and lotions and a fluffy robe emblazoned with the hotel logo. Perry pulled out her phone and snapped a few pictures of the largess and texted them to Campbell.

What's with the fancy digs?

She shoved her phone in her pocket and stowed her bag in the wardrobe. She took one last look at the waste of space and started toward the door when her phone buzzed with a reply.

Thought you could use a little pampering after what you've been through. Enjoy yourself. It's on me.

Perry started typing a response, but she only got a few words out before backspacing to modulate her initial annoyance. She started again and then stopped several times before she finally picked up the phone and dialed.

"Hey, you," Campbell said in her usual chipper voice despite the fact it was o'dark thirty in Austin.

"Hey."

"Are you okay?"

"Of course. Why do you keep asking that?"

"I don't know. Maybe it's not such a weird question to ask one's little sister who was just evacuated from a country while under threat of death."

Leave it to Campbell to exaggerate the circumstances. "It wasn't that bad. If you'd lived in countries under severe unrest like I have, you would realize your welcome is never a guarantee. Don't worry, I escaped with all my white, capitalist freedom intact."

Campbell laughed. "Glad to hear it. In the meantime, I'm using my white capitalist freedom to buy you a fancy hotel suite. Don't worry, I don't think a few days in luxury will taint your passion for the downtrodden."

Perry started to make some remark about how free and easy Campbell was with the money they'd received from their parents' death, but she was too worn out and too hungry to get into a debate right now. Besides, Grace was waiting downstairs. "Did you ask Grace to come?"

"No, it was her idea. I guess you've seen her?"

"Yes. She said she has a contact at the embassy."

"She does. She'll take good care of you."

The words had the dual effect of being both inviting and annoying. "I appreciate all of you thinking I can't take care of myself, but other than needing my documents, I'm perfectly capable of taking care of myself."

"Of course," Campbell said. "But it doesn't hurt to have people willing to help you out, right?"

Campbell always did that—made every argument sound so rational that she'd look like a jerk if she didn't agree. "Yeah, sure. Look, I've got to go, Grace is waiting downstairs."

"No worries. Let me know when you've got everything squared away."

"Sure," Perry said, although she had no doubt Grace would keep Campbell updated on her every move.

"And, Perry?"

"Yes?"

"I love you."

Perry knew it was true, no matter how much Campbell nagged her about their differences. "I know. Me too."

She took a second to check her reflection in the mirror to make sure she didn't look like a total vagabond. Several pieces of hair were jutting out at odd angles in a way that could conceivably be called trendy, but which she knew was merely the result of her lack of skill with a pair of scissors. Her cargo shorts were a bit wrinkled and her I'm the Nasty Woman You've Been Looking For T-shirt had a couple of small holes from wear, but nothing she couldn't hide with her jacket. She was clean and alive and she had her freedom. Grace would either be okay with how she looked or she wouldn't.

She remembered being a kid, sneaking into Campbell's closet and stealing her designer jeans in an effort to impress Grace. Now, years later, she'd apparently grown out of the crush because Grace was taking her to lunch and she didn't care about impressing her. Mostly.

CHAPTER FOUR

Grace looked up from the magazine and sucked in a breath. Twenty-five-year-old Perry Clark was a completely different person than the kid who'd followed her and Campbell around years ago. Some things hadn't changed. Based on the work she did and her reluctance to accept help, she was likely the same rebellious, hardheaded kid she'd been years ago, but her entire appearance had changed. She'd grown into her once gangly and awkward long legs and tall body, and now she strode through the lobby with loads of confidence that came from being lithe and handsome. Staring at Perry's spiky hair fade and piercing brown eyes, Grace realized grown-up Perry was a force, and she recalibrated her strategy about getting her to agree to come home. This would take as much finesse as a corporate merger.

She stood as Perry approached. "How hungry are you?"

"I'm vegetarian."

"Uh, okay. I'm not sure that answers the question, but good to know."

Perry scowled. "I wanted to get that out there right away before you drag me to some place where they serve dead flesh."

Grace laughed. "So, I'm guessing a Sunday roast is not in my future?"

"Oh, it can be in your future, but I won't be joining you unless they have a veggie option." Perry frowned. "Wait, do you think it's going to take that long to get my passport?"

Grace silently chastised herself for referencing time in any way. It was Wednesday, and her plan was to get Perry on a plane to Austin by the end of the week, but her best bet for a sneak attack was to be as vague as possible. She shrugged. "I don't know. We'll talk to my friend tomorrow and find out what we can."

"Besides, it's not like you'd have to wait around. Once you hook me up with your contact, I can take it from there."

"Maybe I'd like to see the city while I'm here. You know, do some touristy things."

"Don't you need to get back to work?"

Grace cocked her head. "If I didn't know better, I'd think you were trying to get rid of me." She tucked Perry's arm under hers. "Let's eat and then make plans. Like Campbell says, food makes it easier to think."

Perry laughed. "She does say that and she's not wrong. Okay with you if I pick the place?"

"Absolutely."

They left the hotel and walked a few blocks. Grace realized she'd brought exactly the wrong shoes and made a mental note to find a new pair as soon as they'd eaten.

"Are you okay back there?"

Grace hid a grimace. "Sure. Overnight on the plane must've left me out of shape."

"You're probably exhausted. You didn't take a nap when you got to the hotel, did you?"

"Not a chance. I read it's the worst thing you can do."

"The place I want to go is a bit of a hike. Are you sure you're up for it?"

Grace weighed her options. She wanted to put on a strong face and act like she could keep up, and on a day she hadn't traveled halfway around the world she could, but there was no sense pretending when it was likely she'd fall over dead before they reached their destination. "I'm totally up for it. The destination, not the hike. How about I spring for an Uber?"

Perry frowned. "An Uber, really?"

"Uh, yes." She held up her phone. "Quick, easy. Faster to the food."

"If you want to put food in the mouths of millionaires at the expense of hardworking people. Besides, I thought they lost their license to operate here."

"I checked. It's on appeal. And I'm pretty sure the hardworking people get paid to work for them, plus they're independent contractors. They get to set their own hours, work when and if they want."

"Sure, it sounds great until you scratch below the surface. The average Uber driver spends more than they make the first year with their initial investment in the type of car the company wants them to drive and extras like water bottles—don't get me started on that—and snacks to win extra stars on their ratings from consumers who don't give a rat's ass if they're making a living wage as long as they can get a ride at the punch of a button. Consumerism at its finest."

Every ounce of Grace's attorney brain wanted to argue the point, but Campbell's voice echoed in her brain, asking her to convince Perry to come back to Austin. She wasn't going to make any headway with typical adversarial moves. She'd have to find another way. In the meantime, if she didn't eat soon, she wouldn't be able to convince anyone of anything. "Let's compromise. How about the Tube? You have any moral objections to riding on an underground train packed with tons of people?"

Perry grinned. "None. And it's much more energy efficient than one car carting the two of us across town." She pointed to a sign on the right. "Here you go."

Grace followed Perry down the narrow stairs to the bustling station. She insisted on buying their tickets, but once they reached the platform, she ceded power to Perry to navigate to their destination. Once on the train, she was grateful to find an open seat where she leaned against the frame and let her eyes fall shut for a moment.

"It's our stop."

Grace sighed at the soft voice and gentle nudge. "Umkay," she murmured, enjoying the comforting envelope of darkness that encircled her like a cocoon.

"Grace, can you wake up for me?"

Grace's eyes fluttered open, but everything was blurry. She rubbed her eyes until they adjusted to the light, and bemoaned the cozy darkness she'd enjoyed a moment before. She was leaning against Perry's shoulder, and at the realization, she immediately straightened in her seat. "What's happening?"

"You're on a train and we're headed to lunch. Are you still up for it?"

"Of course." Grace smiled to cover a suspicion she'd been drooling. She couldn't remember sleeping this hard since the night after the bar exam. "Are we there yet?"

"Next stop."

When they emerged from underground, the street was bustling with people, many of them tourists judging by the variety of accents, venturing in and out of the colorful shops lining the street. "Are you going to give me a hint about where we're going?"

"Sure," Perry said. "Here's your hint. There will be lots of choices."

Grace had meticulously researched London restaurants on the plane ride over. Not that she anticipated getting to indulge much during her stay, but one could hope. She named a couple in case her tastes intersected with Perry's.

"Let me guess," Perry said. "You read those off the top five from *Food & Wine*. Am I right?" She shook her head. "You wanted touristy, that's what you're getting." She pointed up ahead. "There's our destination."

Grace looked up and spotted a large structure suspended from the street with the words Camden Lock in bright yellow. She glanced to her left at the large brick building where a surge of people were climbing stairs. "The market?"

"The very one." Perry pointed at the stairs. "You ready?"

"Absolutely." Grace took the lead and headed up the stairs. London markets were on her list as a close second to historical sites and Michelin-starred restaurants, and Camden was on everyone's short list. "Aren't there like sixty food stalls here? That's state fair level foodie. I'm ravenous." When Perry didn't reply, she looked back to find she'd stopped and was staring at her with a curious expression. "What?"

"Nothing. I guess a part of me thought you might be disappointed we weren't going to a fancy place."

Grace reached back and held out her hand. "You don't know me very well then. Some of the most successful restauranteurs started out in food halls. They are the training ground of the food elite. Food stalls are my kryptonite."

"You'd never know it to look at you."

Perry blushed deep following the compliment, and Grace felt the warmth of a flush under her own skin. If any other woman had said those words, she would've known they were flirting, but coming from the kid sister of her best friend, she knew that couldn't be the case. "You're so sweet." She glanced away to hide a wince at the silly sounding words and waved toward the food vendors set up outside. "Come on, let's eat."

Twenty minutes later, they secured a seat at one of the outdoor picnic tables and surveyed the items they'd gathered—fettuccine Alfredo constructed inside a giant parmesan rind, churros, falafel, and a curried vegetable wrap.

"You didn't get any meat," Perry observed.

"Maybe this is just the first round," Grace said with a grin. "Besides, I figured we could put all this in the middle of the table and share if you don't mind eating with a flesh-eating heathen."

"Very funny." Perry pushed her food to the center. "Help yourself. If I eat all of this, I might never be able to walk again."

Grace did help herself to the falafel, and used the time chewing to really take in Perry. She was slim like she'd always been, but the lanky kid had been replaced by a trim, well-toned woman, and she settled into her space with a confidence Grace had faked at her age. "Tell me what it was like in Crimea?"

Perry set down the bowl of Alfredo and wiped her mouth. "What do you want to know?"

"Anything you care to share."

"The country itself is gorgeous. White beaches, crystal blue sea, mountain slopes, ancient ruins. Everything a tourist could want, and there's plenty of them."

"Sounds like perfection, but I'm sensing there's something you're not telling me."

Perry sighed. "You're right about that. Yes, it's a beautiful place. On the surface. But ever since Russia took over the country, there's a seething darkness just below the surface, poisoning the people left behind when the tourists go home."

"And that's what the journalist, Numeroff, you were representing was trying to expose?"

"Yes, among other things. But freedom of the press is a foreign concept to any place connected to Mother Russia."

"I guess so if they were trying him for high crimes for the simple act of writing a blog. Tell me how Lawyers for Change got involved in his defense. I mean aren't there lawyers in Crimea?"

Grace listened while Perry explained how it was difficult to find in-country representation that wasn't corrupt or ineffective when it came to challenging the government. She was impressed by Perry's passion about her work, and quickly realized it might be harder than she thought to try to convince Perry to return to Austin. No worries—she loved a challenge. She'd simply treat Perry like a case she needed to win. All she had to do was find some leverage she could use, and she'd start right now.

❖

Perry paced outside of Grace's door wondering if she should knock again or return to her own room and wait. She'd checked online and knew the embassy office was already open and she'd considered heading over there herself, but she'd promised Grace she'd wait for her and besides Grace was the one with the contact who might be able to expedite her passport.

They'd spent the rest of the afternoon the day before checking out the vendor stalls at the market until Grace's exhaustion from travel kicked in late in the day and they'd returned to the hotel. By her count, Grace had now been asleep for over twelve hours—way past time to recover from jet lag and in danger of only making it worse. It was practically her duty to wake her, but as she raised her hand to knock on the door, she remembered how cute Grace had looked sound asleep on the Tube, eyes closed and emitting tiny snores no one else could possibly hear but which had been endearing all the same. Watching Grace slumber, Perry's childhood crush had come roaring back, likely a by-product of the vacation vibe from their day's adventures.

But today she was back to the practicalities of life. It was time to get her papers in order so she could rejoin her group and Grace could go home to whatever corporate debacle needed her attention. She rapped on the door before she could change her mind.

"Coming," Grace called out from within.

Perry paced outside the door until Grace appeared. To her surprise, Grace was dressed and Perry spotted a cart with the remains of a meal behind her. "You had breakfast?"

Grace looked sheepish. "I did. I woke up starving and I didn't want to bother you, so I ordered room service. If you want to go get something, I could join you for coffee."

"Actually, I'd rather just head to the embassy. In fact, if I can get my birth certificate from you, I can go on my own."

"Uh, okay." Grace glanced behind her. "You sure you're not hungry?"

"Positive." It was a lie. She was starving, but she cared more about getting a passport than food and she could eat once she was done at the embassy. "Like I said, you don't have to babysit me." She instantly regretted the words when she saw the hurt expression on Grace's face. "I know you're trying to help, but I also know you probably have other things to do here or you wouldn't have traipsed all the way across the pond. I appreciate the hand-delivery, but I'm officially letting you know you're off the hook. Okay?" Again with the slighted look, and Perry wondered why her offer had offended Grace. "I mean you can come if you want, but you don't have to."

Grace grabbed her phone and keycard from the counter and pointed at the door. "Let's go."

Perry led the way out of the hotel to the nearest Tube station with Grace on her heels. Once they were on the train, she asked, "Did you get a good night's sleep?"

"I did. The blackout curtains were the perfect remedy to my mixed-up body clock. How about you?"

Perry shook her head. "Not sure why, but it may be that the room's a little big for just one person. I spent the last few months living in a space half that size with two other people. I think I felt a little…" She paused searching for the right word. "I don't know. Exposed, maybe. Does that make sense?"

Grace cocked her head. "It does. And based on what Campbell has told me, you've been living in Spartan conditions. I'm sure she thought the suite would be a welcome change."

"I get it. Yeah, our accommodations in Crimea and Afghanistan before that were more third world than first, but I've become used to living with less." She met Grace's eyes and tried to read the expression reflected back at her. Sympathy? Curiosity? Whatever it was, she wanted to change the subject to something that would take the focus off of her. "So, it sounds like you know all about my exploits. What have you been up to in Austin? Dating anyone special?" She instantly regretted the question when she saw the sad look on Grace's face. "Not that it's any of my business."

"No," Grace said. "It's not that. Campbell and Abby are constantly on me for not getting out there and dating more, and I get where they're coming from since they're both smitten with their girlfriends. I have been dating more since I left big law, but more is relative and I haven't met anyone who I was interested in sticking with past the first couple of dates."

Perry thought she spotted a wistful look in Grace's eye and she wondered what that was about. Grace was a catch. A prize-winning, trophy on the mantel kind of catch, and she shouldn't settle for anyone who didn't understand her value and live up to it, but she hesitated to tell her so for fear she'd come off like that gushing kid who'd snuck around the house to catch glimpses of Grace every time she showed up to hang out with Campbell. No, she was way past silly crushes, and as attractive and accomplished as Grace was, they were completely different people now and probably always had been. "Well, I'm sure the right woman will show up any time now," she said, settling on a silly platitude.

"What about you?" Grace said. "Does life on the run leave time for dating?"

"Dating?" Perry shook her head. "Not even."

"But there's something," Grace said. "Let me guess, a woman in every country?"

Perry felt the burn of a blush creep up her neck as she remembered yesterday morning's predawn sex with Linda. But that wasn't dating. Dating was a path to something else. What she had with Linda, or anyone else for that matter, was nothing more than no strings attached, in the moment fun. No expectations and no future, leaving her free to pursue whatever opportunities life would throw her way. Which meant Grace's assessment was spot-on. Then why did it make her feel uncomfortable to have Grace say it out loud? She shrugged, deciding it was best to own the characterization. "Yep, that's me. Love 'em and leave 'em."

Grace stared at her for a second, like she was trying to assess how serious she was and then broke the gaze. "The embassy should be right around this corner."

Strangely sad, but mostly relieved the conversation was back to business, Perry sped up and strode in front of Grace to reach the building. "What's your friend's name?" she said, looking back at Grace.

"Jeff Harmon. Let me talk to him first before you go charging in there." Grace stepped in front of her, motioned for her to wait, and approached the guard.

Perry watched the exchange, at first chafing a bit over being left out, and then settled into enjoying Grace in take-charge mode, but when Grace disappeared farther into the building, she started to feel fidgety on her own in the midst of all of the armed personnel. When she caught the guard eyeing her, she turned and headed back out of the building. The level of official authority in the building gave her the willies. She'd give Grace fifteen minutes and then she was on to plan B, whatever that was.

CHAPTER FIVE

Grace greeted Jeff Harmon, the deputy chief of public affairs, with a big hug. She'd met Jeff when she'd volunteered on President Meredith Mitchell's first campaign. When Mitchell had soared to victory, Jeff took a job at the state department and scored this dream placement soon after.

"How's your father doing?" Jeff asked. "Still champion of the underdog?"

"You know it." Grace smiled to cover a mild annoyance that everyone she knew mentioned her father the senator every time they met, like he was a currency they traded back and forth. The truth was, she could've called his office and asked one of his staffers to contact the embassy about Perry's passport, but there was no guarantee he'd help, and it was easier to handle it herself than ask and be rebuffed. She could hear him now: How can I take a hard line against corruption if I grant favors to my family and friends? He needn't have worried since she couldn't remember the last time he'd treated her any differently than one of the many others who'd helped elect him to the Senate and she'd learned not to expect any special treatment from him.

"He and Mom have been spending a lot of this term in DC," she said. "I haven't seen them much, but I'm sure he'll be making a trip back after the next recess. Mom prefers to be in Texas for the summer. She says while the heat is the same as DC, it's only half as humid."

"I do not miss the heat." Jeff invited her to sit down. "Now that we've discussed the weather, let me see if I can help you. Tell me what you need."

Grace sat on the edge of the chair and launched in. "Perry is my best friend's sister and she's stubborn as hell. She's been practicing law with an NGO in underserved aka hotbed areas, and they had to leave their last one so quickly, she lost her passport in the process."

"I'm guessing, this last hotbed wasn't here in the UK?"

"It wasn't." Grace raised a hand, palm out, hoping he didn't ask which country they were talking about. "Don't ask me how she got here without a passport. I don't know and I don't think either of us want to know. But she needs a new one so she can resume travel as quickly as possible."

"The normal process is for her to complete a form swearing to the circumstances under which she lost her current passport. I'm guessing you don't want her to have to answer a bunch of extra questions?"

"What I want is, I mean what her sister wants, is for her to come home to Austin as soon as possible and settle down for a while. If you could issue her an emergency passport that she could use to travel back to the US, then we'd have time to convince her to stick around and stay out of these kinds of scrapes. I know I'm asking a lot here, and I totally get it if you can't make it happen."

"Actually, I can make it happen." He grinned. "You may be a big shot lawyer, but I've got a few important connections. As long as you vouch for Perry and promise to stick to her like glue until she's back in the States, we could get her an emergency passport as quickly as tomorrow."

"That would be fantastic," Grace said, hoping she sounded enthusiastic. She'd kind of hoped the process would take a few more days to give her time to both explore London and warm Perry up to the idea of accompanying her back to Austin. "What do we need to do?"

"I'll need proof of a booked flight back home. You'll need her passport number to do that, but I can get that for you if she doesn't remember it. Once I have that, I'll rush this through and if all goes well, I can have it ready for you in the morning. You can spend the rest of the day exploring the city."

Grace held up her phone. "I'll book the flight right now. I owe you for this."

"How about dinner tonight? The ambassador is hosting the prime minister for a shindig tonight. Any chance you want to be my plus-one? I can't promise it won't be stuffy, but the chef here is next level so at least the food will be good."

Grace opened her mouth to say absolutely, but then memory kicked in and she felt silly for almost forgetting she'd left Perry in the lobby. Any other time, she would've loved to attend an embassy function with highbrow food and the chance to rub shoulders with people in power—people who would send business to the firm—but she'd promised Campbell she'd keep Perry in her sights until she was back in Austin. "I'd love to, but I've already got a commitment for tonight."

"Raincheck for next time you're in London?"

"Absolutely. And if you're ever in Austin and need a favor, let me know."

Back in the lobby, Grace spotted Perry leaning against a counter with her legs crossed, like she didn't have a care in the world, and again Grace couldn't help but notice she was nothing like the gangly kid who used to follow her and Campbell around, practically begging them to include her in whatever they were doing. They'd rebuffed her most of the time, telling her they were doing grown-up things and she was just a little girl. Grace let her gaze roam over the confident young woman Perry had become and realized she was all grown-up now, but hopefully not so grown-up that she couldn't be persuaded to come back to Austin. She merely had to find the right moment to broach the subject.

Perry looked up as she approached, her eyes questioning. "How did it go? How long do I have to wait? Do they need to talk to me?"

Grace smiled at her eagerness even though she knew the real purpose behind Perry's anxiousness to get her passport was the exact opposite of what she needed to convince her to do. She motioned to the door, deciding it was best that if there was going to be a confrontation, that it happen outside the walls of the embassy. Once they were clear of the gate, she turned to Perry. "Okay, I have some good news and some other good news."

"That sounds suspiciously like you have good news for me and good news for someone else."

Mildly impressed with Perry's ability to see through her opening, Grace pressed on. "The first piece of good news is that you should have a new passport by tomorrow."

"That is better than good. It's fantastic," Perry said. "I was scared it was going to take much longer."

"It would've under other circumstances, but we worked out an agreement."

"And this is where I hold my breath while you tell me the other news."

Grace sighed. "You're booked on a flight with me back to Austin Friday morning. Now that isn't so bad, is it?"

"Austin?" Perry shook her head. "Not in the plan. Not even remotely on the way to where I plan to go."

"Where exactly do you plan to go?"

"Wherever I'm needed. I should get my new assignment any moment, and as soon as the passport comes through, I'll be heading out."

"It doesn't work like that," Grace said, barely trying to hide the exasperation in her voice. She'd used up a big favor with Jeff and who knows if she'd ever need his help for anything again, yet Perry was so quick to brush it off like it was nothing. She was tempted to tell her just that before she remembered she was supposed to be cajoling Perry, not pissing her off. "Booking a flight back to the States is how I was able to get you a new passport without you having to answer a bunch of questions, like for example about how you entered this country illegally. It's also the only way I was able to get them to expedite it."

Perry huffed, but Grace could see her brain was whirring. "Fine," she said. "I'll fly to Austin, but I'm booking the next flight out of there."

Grace wanted to point out all the reasons it would make more sense for Perry to spend some time in Austin, reconnecting with Campbell and her brother, and figuring out a plan for her future, but the fierce expression on Perry's face told her now wasn't the time to push. Getting her to agree to go home, even if only to the airport, was the first step. She had twenty-four hours to seal the deal. The best thing she could do right now was pretend it didn't matter what Perry decided to do. "Well, we've got a day to kill. Feel like sightseeing with me? We can each pick one thing. I'll do whatever you want."

"What if you pick something boring and paternalistic like the Tower of London?"

"What if you pick something silly like hopping on and off one of those double-decker buses packed with tourists?" Grace smiled. "Look, it's a risk for both of us, but you're guaranteed at least fifty percent of a good time, and I'll spring for dinner tonight. What do you say?" She waited, hoping Perry would agree to the plan rather than going back to her room to pout about having been outmaneuvered into returning to Austin even if only for a connecting flight. Perry had every right to feel disappointed at the detour in her plans, but Grace was going to be disappointed too if they didn't get to spend the day together. More than she would've expected. If she was left to explore London on her own, she would, but the idea of seeing the sights without Perry left Grace feeling inexplicably empty and a little bit agitated as a result.

"Fine. Let's do it."

Grace didn't bother trying to contain her grin. This was going to be an epic day.

❖

Perry grinned at Grace who was staring up into the sky. "What's the matter?"

"Nothing, if you have a death wish."

They were standing in front of the entrance to the Eye, the giant, fully enclosed Ferris wheel on the River Thames. "I know it's not a fancy museum or a palace, but I have a thing for Ferris wheels and this is like the Super Bowl of Ferris wheels."

"There's something really off about that analogy and I'll figure it out when I'm not feeling like I'm going to throw up."

Perry laughed. "We haven't even been up in the air yet. All thirty-plus stories of air." She tugged on Grace's arm. "Come on. The website says you can see everything from up there. It's like a bonus round of sightseeing." She assumed a pleading expression. "Besides, you promised."

Grace sighed. "I did. And I keep my promises even if it means dying in the process."

Perry let her hand slip down and grasp Grace's, enjoying the feel of their fingers entwined for a moment before she remembered her crush was in the past and Grace was only here to escort her back to Austin. She gave her a quick squeeze and let go. "I won't let you die. That's my promise."

"Well, I hope not because I have something very special planned for my half of the day."

Before boarding, they paused for a quick selfie with a perky blond ride operator who chatted Perry up about where she was from and what she did for a living, and then insisted on holding the camera in order to get the best angle. As they were boarding, Perry examined her phone and found Grace was almost completely cut out of the picture. "Well, that sucks."

Grace leaned in to look. "I'm not surprised."

"What?"

"She was totally flirting with you. If we'd spent more time with her, she might've pushed me off the platform."

"Over my dead body."

"Look how gallant you are," Grace said. "But I'm pretty sure it would be more like over mine."

Perry frowned and shook her head. The idea of the ride operator flirting with her in front of Grace made her uncomfortable and she didn't know why. "I'm sorry."

Grace laughed. "Don't be silly. She's cute."

"Not my type."

Grace arched an eyebrow. "Really? What is your type?"

Okay, so it was getting really warm in the car. Perry fanned herself and looked around for a convenient distraction. She pressed against the glass. "There's Parliament," she said, pointing in the distance. "And there's Big Ben."

"Uh-huh."

Perry looked back over her shoulder at Grace who was standing in the middle of the car, strategically far from any of the windows. "Hey, you," she called out. "You're missing all the fun."

"I'm good."

"Seriously, Grace." Perry held out her hand. "I got you." She watched as Grace walked toward her. She'd never known Grace to be afraid of anything, so this whole display was a bit of a wonder, and she puffed up a little at the idea she had assumed the role as the stronger one, in this situation anyway. When Grace reached her side, she slipped a hand around her waist. "If you tumble out, I'm going with you."

Grace frowned. "I don't find that particularly reassuring."

"Then how about we both stay safe? You can start by relaxing and enjoying the sights." She pointed in the distance. "Look, there's the Shard."

"You're a regular tour guide. I thought you'd never been to London before."

"I haven't." Perry hesitated, not entirely sure she wanted to say more, and if she were with anyone but Grace, she would have made up some reason why she was obsessed with all the sights. "Mom and Dad honeymooned in Europe, and London was my mom's favorite place on the trip. You remember she had those salt and pepper shakers that looked like the royal guard? Purchased right here in jolly old England."

"I remember," Grace said. "They didn't go with the rest of the decor at your house at all. I figured they had some sentimental value."

Perry nodded. "They always talked about coming back to visit one day, but they never seemed to find the time to make the trip."

She glanced off at a spot in the distance, willing herself not to cry as she swallowed the lump in her throat. It had been a little over fifteen years since her parents died. They'd been taking a helicopter tour of New York City, and the combination of a mechanical failure and an intoxicated pilot sent the craft plummeting from the sky without warning, killing everyone on board. The subsequent lawsuit and settlement had set Perry and her siblings up for life, but she'd give back every cent for another day with her folks. She felt Grace squeeze her hand and she looked up to find her staring with a gentle gaze.

"I'm so sorry you lost them. They were the best."

"They were, weren't they?"

"Yep," Grace said. "And the least I can do is lean in and enjoy the sights on their behalf. Would your mom have liked this contraption?"

Perry smiled as she remembered her mother's enthusiasm for rides of any kind, from slow-moving Ferris wheels to rocketing roller coasters. "Hell yes. Plus, she loved riding on top of the double-decker buses, but this would be exponentially better." She swept her arm in a broad gesture in front of the glass. "You have to admit, it is pretty cool to be able to see the entire city out in front of you."

"It is pretty cool. Enjoy it while you can. My portion of the day will provide a completely different perspective."

"Is that so?" Perry asked, curious about what Grace had in store. "Care to drop a hint?"

"Sure. It involves wheels, but much smaller ones than this contraption."

Perry pointed at the window where their car was approaching ground level. "Looks like you're about to be free from the contraption." A moment later, Perry held Grace's arm as they exited the ride into a kitschy gift store. To her surprise, Grace was like a kid in a candy shop picking through all of the selections.

"Are you looking for something specific?"

Grace looked up from a stuffed bear holding a Union Jack. "Whatever will vault me to the spot of aunt of the year. My niece just turned eight. To be honest, I have absolutely no clue what an eight-year-old girl would like."

Perry pulled a snapback hat emblazoned with the word London off a rack and examined it. "Depends on the girl, I guess. If she's kind of girly, like Campbell, then maybe that brush and mirror set, but if she's a tomboy, then a pocketknife or a wallet." She put on the cap. "Or this fine headgear."

Grace laughed. "You aren't seriously going to buy that are you?"

Perry posed with her arms crossed. "What's the matter? You don't like it?"

"If you want to tell the world you're a tourist, be my guest." Grace grinned and grabbed the same hat in a different color. "Maybe I'll join you." She assumed the same pose. "How do I look?"

Silly hat aside, breathtaking was the first word that came to mind, but Perry caught herself before she spoke. "Selfie worthy. Pic?" She held her breath as Grace slipped an arm around her waist and they posed for the camera. After she'd snapped the photo, they both stared at the screen and Perry was pleased to see not a single one of Grace's attributes had been cut out. They looked good together, and a stranger looking at the photo might think they were a couple.

She shook away the thought. There was a time when she'd dreamed of being in Grace's arms, but those were the fantasies of youth. Fantasies were for children. The affection Grace was showing her now was exactly the same as when she used to rub her on the head and tell her she was a good kid, no matter how it looked in a photo.

❖

Grace pointed at the row of bicycles and grinned at Perry. "See? Wheels, but the kind that stay on the ground."

Perry's eyes narrowed. "What is happening right now?"

Grace took a moment to take in the scene. They were in an alley of sorts next to a pub. The alley was lined with a dozen retro-style bicycles, complete with sweet little baskets, and, standing in front of the bikes was a tall, thin, older gentlemen wearing a tweed driver's cap and checked pants and a vest explaining the rules of the road. She turned back to Perry and motioned between them. "You, me, gin, markets, all the sights. We're going on a bicycle tour."

A slow smile spread across Perry's face and she looked as eager as she had when they'd boarded the Eye. "Heck yeah, we are. What a great idea."

"Not too stodgy?"

"Well, aside from the Oliver Twist looking guy standing over there, not stodgy at all. Do we get to pick which bike we want?"

Grace watched as Perry surveyed the bicycles, proud she'd picked an activity they would both enjoy, and glad the tour had a couple of last-minute openings. After the great time they'd had at Camden Market, she knew they'd have fun on this tour. Plus, there would be gin.

An hour later, they'd seen the Tate Museum, the oldest church in London, the Shard, and they'd narrowly avoided getting smacked by a bus that cut between the two of them and the rest of the cyclists on the tour.

"And you thought the Eye was dangerous," Perry shouted from behind Grace.

"You want to take the lead?" Grace slowed down, acutely conscious of the fact Perry was behind her and she figured she was chomping at the bit to go faster. She waved her arm. "Go on, lead the way."

Perry pulled ahead, her legs pumping and her face wearing a broad smile. "This was the best idea ever," she called out as she whizzed by. "When do we get to the next market?"

Before she could answer, Perry shouted, "Where's the rest of the group?"

Grace looked around but didn't see any of the other cyclists or their tour guide. "Pull up over there for a second," she said, motioning to a line of hedges. She followed Perry up on the sidewalk, certain the group couldn't be far away. She was just starting to slow down when a couple walking down the sidewalk abruptly turned to face her. The woman shook her fist in the air. "Get off the sidewalk. You're breaking the law!"

The shout took her by surprise and Grace nearly fell off her bike. She felt an arm reach out to steady her and looked up to see Perry standing next to her.

"I've got you."

Time suspended and the noise of the city fell away. For a second, they were simply two women, far away from home, connected by love of adventure and the comfortable ease of having known each other most of their lives. But for the shouting locals and the stomach lurching heights of the Eye, Grace would consider this a perfect date. Oh, and if Perry weren't her best friend's little sister. But she was, so Grace slowly backed out of Perry's embrace and swiftly changed the subject. "Did that really just happen?"

Perry raised her fist in the air. "You mean the part where you were breaking the law!" she said, over-exaggerating the war cry of the angry local. "Yep. Grace Maldonado, chief rule follower and barrister of great renown, was just accused of violating the laws of a foreign land."

They both doubled over in laughter. When the gales of laughter finally faded, Grace asked, "What do you mean, chief rule follower?"

Perry furrowed her brow. "Come on, admit it. You're like the high priestess of regulations."

"Am not."

"Are too. Why do you think Campbell and Abby made you the managing partner of the firm?"

A bunch of reasons popped in her head, but they all supported Perry's general proposition that she was the most responsible one, so she didn't bother listing them. "Okay then, I'm going to take that as a compliment. Rules are good. They keep order in the universe."

"Sure, but people find ways to bend them all the time in the name of whatever order they prefer. People of privilege anyway. I've been working in areas of the world where privilege doesn't exist and rules don't matter unless you're white and privileged. And rich. Rich really helps."

Grace started to point out that the only one in this conversation who was white was Perry and they were both privileged by virtue of where they'd grown up and their families, but instead she bit her tongue and let Perry ruminate for a moment to see if she came to the same conclusion.

"I'm sorry. That came out wrong," Perry said. "There's so much injustice in the world that it swallows me up sometimes."

"I get it," Grace said. "I really do. But if you dwell on it, you're going to be consumed." She pointed at Perry's bike. "Now get back on that thing because today the rule follower is throwing all caution to the wind. I'm going to drink gin and eat fun foods and maneuver this bike around the streets of London like a pro. Are you with me?"

Perry answered by straddling her bike and ringing the bell. "I am absolutely with you." She pointed at the road ahead. "If you can catch up with me."

And just like that, an idea popped into Grace's head. "If you're up for a challenge, I've got one for you."

"Bring it."

The eagerness in Perry's voice told Grace she had her hooked. She pointed at a spot in the distance. "I'll race you to that corner up there. If I win, you'll stay in Austin."

Perry cocked her head to the side. "For how long?"

"A week," Grace said, figuring she wouldn't go for anything longer, but a week should give Campbell enough time to make her case to convince Perry to stay.

"What happens when I win?"

"Hell freezes over," Grace said, fixing her face into a perfect deadpan. "If indeed such a cataclysmic event happens, then when we land in Austin, I will personally book your flight to wherever you want and use my contacts to speed up the issuance of your new permanent passport."

Perry narrowed her eyes, like she was considering the proposal, and then without warning, she pushed away from the hedge and sped off. Grace watched her go, wanting to take a moment to savor the moment, but then she pumped the pedals hard because she had to win this race.

Chapter Six

G race stirred at the sound of the meal cart trundling through the aisle and she slowly stretched. She hadn't planned to sleep on the plane, it was a daytime flight after all, but once she'd reclined the seat, all bets were off. She glanced at the time and saw that they were about an hour from landing in Austin. She looked back and saw Perry, a row back and across the aisle, headphones in, watching something on her iPad with rapt attention. When the flight attendant stopped at her seat, Grace begged off the snack, asking for coffee instead. When he passed on by, she grabbed her bag and headed to the bathroom to freshen up. On the way back, she heard a familiar voice behind her.

"Hello again."

She turned to see Danika, the tall blonde she'd met on the flight to London. The flirty one. "Hello yourself."

"I've been waiting all this time to buy you a Manhattan, but I didn't want to wake you."

Suddenly self-conscious at the idea of Danika watching her sleep, Grace fumbled for words. "Crazy, right? I don't know why I'm so sleepy today, but once the roar of the engines started, I sacked right out. Are you headed home?"

Danika nodded and motioned to the snack area and they both stepped in. "I am. I assume you are too. Did you accomplish everything you intended on your trip?"

Why did her words seem to carry so much extra meaning? Grace started to answer when the purpose for her trip piped up behind her.

"Hey, Grace, are you finally awake?" Perry called out as she approached. "Guess the bike ride wore you out, huh?" Perry looked from Danika back to her with a curious expression, and then stuck out her hand. "Hi, I'm Perry Clark."

Danika shot Grace a quick arch of her eyebrows and shook Perry's hand. "Danika Larsen."

Grace watched the exchange and scrambled to explain. "Perry is my law partner's sister. I was helping her out with a travel document issue, and now we're both headed back to Austin."

Grace spotted a frown shadow Perry's face. She looked back at Danika and saw a slow smile spread across her face, full of portent.

"That's fantastic news." Danika leaned in closer. "If you still have my card, give me a call sometime. I'd love to buy you that Manhattan when we're on level ground."

As she edged away, Grace turned back to Perry. "I can't believe I slept the entire flight."

"I can't believe you're angling for a hookup while we're in the middle of the Atlantic."

"Very funny."

"I'm being serious. That woman was undressing you with her eyes."

"'Undressing me with her eyes?' Who talks like that? And for your information, we're not over the Atlantic anymore, we're over dry land and almost back in Austin."

"Just looking out for you. You shouldn't be talking to strangers."

"She's not a stranger. We've met before." Grace didn't add that the first meeting had been on the flight to London. Perry's patronizing tone was already annoying without her knowing the full story. "I promise you I'm perfectly capable of taking care of myself."

"Sure, whatever." Perry stuck her hands in her pockets and shifted in place.

"What's up?"

"Did you already tell Campbell I'm going to stick around for a while?"

Uh-oh. "You're not trying to back out on our agreement are you?"

"No, a bet's a bet." She shrugged. "I just didn't have time to figure out a place to stay. I want to have my act together before I show up at her place like a vagabond with no place to go."

"Well, there won't be much time for that since she insisted on picking us up at the airport." Grace held up her hands. "Don't get mad. She'd already insisted on picking me up, so she's not making a special trip for you, but would that really be a bad thing?"

Perry sighed. "I guess not. She's never been a fan of these trips and there's going to be a lot of I told you sos."

"Give her a chance. She misses you and it means a lot to her that you're staying for a while. You know how she is. She feels like she needs to keep you close because…" Grace struggled to find an ending to the sentence that wasn't insensitive.

"I know and I get it, but we all lead very different lives. Austin doesn't equal home to me, and it hasn't for a long time. And pretending we're a regular happy family has never worked no matter how Pollyanna Campbell wants to be."

Grace felt a twinge of guilt for pushing Perry to return, when it was clearly painful for her to do so, but she'd made a promise to Campbell who was in a much better position to decide what was best for her family. "Tell you what. If things get to be too much, call me. Anytime. We'll go have gin cocktails and ride bikes, although not necessarily at the same time. Deal?"

"Deal."

The captain's voice came over the speaker, instructing them to return to their seats to prepare for landing. Grace watched Perry settle back in, while she waited until the last possible moment before taking her seat. She knew in her heart she'd done the right thing by convincing Perry to come back to Austin, but she doubted Perry would stay longer than the week she'd promised. Oh well, it wasn't her problem anymore. It was up to Campbell now to convince her to stay, but she'd meant what she told Perry about being there for her, and after the fun they'd had in London, she secretly hoped Campbell would succeed.

❖

Perry stood in the living room of her sister's new house. It was her first time seeing the place and she took a moment to note both the familiar and unfamiliar. The mantel over the fireplace contained pictures of both her and their brother and their parents, along with framed photos of several people Perry didn't recognize. The furniture was stylish, yet it looked comfortable and inviting, and several of the knickknacks and art pieces scattered around the room didn't fit with what she remembered about her taste, but the fancy TV and surround-sound system were pure Campbell.

"Make yourself at home," Campbell said, handing her a bottle of water. "You must be exhausted."

Home. A familiar word with no particular meaning anymore. The last few years, her home had taken various forms from a crash pad with her law school buddies to a tent in the deserts of the Middle East to the cramped quarters in the back of a small office in Crimea. Campbell's house was the Taj Mahal in comparison, and while many people might find that comforting, the extravagant comfort only made her anxious. Perry looked down at the bottle in Campbell's hand. "I'm good, thanks."

Campbell hesitated, like she wanted to insist, but thought better of it. "Well, have a seat anyway."

Perry settled onto the couch, but stayed on the edge, ready to make a quick getaway if things got awkward. "Where's Wynne?" she asked, referring to Campbell's fiancée.

"She had a long depo today, but she'll be home later. I figured I could order us some dinner and we could catch up."

"I'm kind of stuffed. I ate like four meals on the plane. You know you didn't have to spring for first class."

Campbell shrugged. "It's a rough flight in coach. I figure you've had plenty of rough times lately and it wouldn't hurt to be spoiled for a bit."

Perry wanted to say that the money that paid for her upgrade would've fed a family of four in a third world country for the better part of a year, but she knew Campbell was a generous person and it would only make her feel bad if she said anything. Besides, as much as she didn't want to admit it, flying first class had made the journey much easier to take. She hadn't truly realized how exhausted she was after the escape from Crimea until she was settled into her pod on the plane back from the UK. "It didn't suck. The hotel suite was a nice touch too. But why do I have a feeling there's a string attached?"

Campbell waved her off. "Don't be silly. It was a small price to pay to make sure you had a chance to relax."

It *was* a small price for Campbell who'd come into her trust last year. "You know, now that you and Justin are the trustees, you could release my money early. Then I could pay for my own hotel rooms and first class tickets."

"More likely you'd buy a village in the middle of some country we've never heard of and build houses for all of the villagers."

Damn, Campbell had her pegged. "And that's a bad thing?"

"Of course not. You know if you're really into pro bono work, there are plenty of people right here in Austin that could use your help."

She was right, but the right here in Austin part was the problem. Perry knew she'd done everything she could do to distance herself from the city since she'd gone away to college, and she knew exactly why. Campbell and Justin might have no problem calling Austin home, but she didn't think there would ever come a time when the memories of happy times with her parents would ever fade sufficiently to allow her to enjoy the city where she'd grown up again. "I'll stick around for a week or so, but then I need to get back to my job."

Campbell stared at her for a moment like she was contemplating saying something else, but decided against it. "Okay. But do you think you can come by the office next week? Abby would love to see you and I want to show you around."

"Sure." It seemed like a small price to pay for having been rescued. Besides, until she got a permanent passport, she wasn't going to be leaving the country anytime soon. "Look, I know this is going to sound rude, but in my head it's a lot later and I'm pretty beat. Would it be okay if I went ahead and turned in for the night and met Wynne tomorrow? I'll feel and look a lot less scraggly then."

"Sure," Campbell said, but there was a trace of disappointment in her eyes. "Come on, I'll show you the guest room."

The room was like the hotel suite at the Savoy, full of all the creature comforts from a large screen TV to a full-sized private bathroom with a Jacuzzi tub. Perry set her worn duffel bag beside the bed. "Between London and here, it's kind of like you're trying to spoil me."

"Maybe you deserve to be spoiled." Campbell's expression softened. "I know you've put your heart and soul into saving the world, but that's not all there is to life. You don't have to be the downtrodden to make the world a better place." She pulled Perry into a hug. "I love you, kid."

"I love you too." Despite her efforts to remain stoic, Perry felt tears well up in her eyes and she shooed Campbell away. "Now get out of here so I can lounge on silk sheets and watch TV on the giant screen. See you in the morning."

After Campbell shut the door behind her, Perry sank onto the bed and contemplated the whirlwind that was her life. A few days ago, she'd been sharing a makeshift bedroom with Linda and giving legal advice to a rebel journalist in Crimea, and now she was ensconced in a large house with nothing to do and anything she wanted at her fingertips. In between, she'd roamed the streets of London with her high school crush who was way hotter and way more enticing than she'd been when she'd first started lusting after her years ago. She had no idea what tomorrow would bring, but if the past week was any indication, anything could happen. She'd better get a good night's sleep if she wanted to be ready for it.

Chapter Seven

Sunday morning, Perry strolled into Campbell's kitchen and spent a full five minutes staring into the fridge before an unfamiliar voice shook her out of her trance.

"If you don't see what you want, add it to the list and I'll make sure to pick it up at the store."

Wishing she'd chosen to put on real clothes, she turned toward the voice, feigning confidence at her sock monkey boxer shorts and tank top. "Either you're a grocery delivery person who reads minds or you're Wynne, my sister's fiancée."

"I could be both, but my name is definitely Wynne." Her smile was warm as she stuck out her hand. "And you're either an escapee from a sleep study or my fiancée's sister, Perry."

"Again, it could be both." Perry smiled, deciding she already liked Wynne. "Nice to meet you. I'd tell you that I usually make a better first impression, but that would be a lie."

"No worries. I'm already impressed with you based on what Campbell's told me. Sorry I missed your big return to town. I've been buried in trial prep. Speaking of work, were you really in Crimea working on Numeroff's case? I follow his blog. Fascinating stuff."

"I was until last week when we went on the run." She hunched her shoulders. "Hazard of the job when you're doing legal work in countries where there aren't a lot of laws to protect regular people who're trying to exercise their rights."

Wynne nodded. "Well, I'm glad you made it out okay and I'm glad we're getting to meet. I know Campbell is happy you're here. I hope we can share a meal soon and hear all about your work. Please say you'll stick around for the wedding."

Wedding. Right. That's what fiancées did. They got married. In a ceremony with dresses and guests and cake and presents. Any excitement Perry felt at the prospect of talking to someone who was actually interested in Numeroff's case vanished at the mention of the looming formal occasion. A big fancy wedding—or any wedding at all—wasn't something she would want, but it was right up Campbell's love of all things traditional romance alley. Perry scrambled for a noncommittal response but knew there was no way she was getting out of attending. Her efforts would be better spent trying to think of something cool to wear before Campbell tried to dress her in some creepy bridesmaid dress. "It's in a month, right?"

"To the day."

"I really want to, but there's a chance I may have to report back to my group before then. We don't get a lot of say in when or where we're assigned."

A flicker of disappointment crossed Wynne's face, and Perry felt a stab of guilt for causing it, but she figured it was better to set realistic expectations up front. She changed the subject to deflect. "I promised Campbell I'd drop by the office this week. Will I see you there?"

"Unlikely. I've been trapped at opposing counsel's office all week in depositions."

"Snore." Perry smiled. She'd never actually sat through a deposition, but she'd listened to plenty of her law school friends recount hours spent listening to the excruciating drib drab of questions and answers during their law firm internships, and the telling made her yawn so she figured the real thing was a snoozefest for sure.

"You're not wrong, but it pays the bills."

"Interesting case at least?"

"Country singer sues social media company for allegedly damaging her reputation."

"I take it from the word 'allegedly' you do not represent the country singer?"

"You are very astute. I knew I was marrying into a smart family."

Perry laughed. She liked Wynne and looked forward to having her join the family. Maybe she should make an effort to attend the wedding…

Wynne rinsed her coffee mug and placed it in the dishwasher. "I better get going."

"Is Campbell still upstairs?"

"No, she ran by the office to handle a couple of things that couldn't wait until tomorrow, but she said she'd be back later this afternoon."

Perry was partly relieved. Campbell had left her alone yesterday so she could get some much needed rest, but by now she was likely dying to give her the third degree about every detail of her escape from Crimea and trip from London. "Okay, well, I guess I'll see you both later."

Perry watched Wynne leave and contemplated her day. She'd made plans for lunch with her brother, Justin, but she still had a couple of hours before she needed to get ready. She contemplated calling Tom to check on the status of his latest post with Lawyers for Change, but if he asked her any questions about her travel status, she didn't have answers to give. If there was one thing she hated more than being in limbo, it was admitting she was in limbo. No sense contacting him until she had solid intel about when she'd be able to travel again. She decided to wait a couple of days and then see if Grace would contact her pal at the state department for a status on her permanent passport.

Grace. The mere thought of her name caused memories of the last couple of days to pop to the surface. She couldn't remember the last time she'd had as much fun, and she laughed out loud at the vision of Grace, weaving in and out of traffic on the bicycle only to be cursed by a raised fist local shouting at her to obey the law. And that was before they'd imbibed their first gin of the day. When she was a kid, she never would've believed that one day she'd be riding around London on a bike with her crush, and the reality had been everything she would've wanted. Except she was an adult now—past crushes and teenage dreams. So, why did she keep coming back to the time they'd spent together and hoping, with a kind of second date infatuation, that Grace would be at the office when she dropped in tomorrow?

Grace opened the door to Clark, Keene, and Maldonado, surprised to see their office manager, Graham, at his desk on a Sunday. He was on the phone and she edged past hoping to get a cup of coffee before he could load her up with details about everything she'd missed while on her jaunt to London, but he hung up before she could reach the door to the inside offices.

"Good morning, Grace," Graham said with a flourish of his hand. "Best of mornings to you. Although, it's actually afternoon in your head, correct?"

"Correct. And I'm feeling it. What are you doing here on a Sunday morning?"

"Humbly offering my services. Campbell mentioned you would be in this morning, and I presumed you would like a full roster of the happenings in your absence."

"If it's all the same to you, I'd like to grab a cup of coffee before we go over anything. You know, give my brain a chance to catch up with the time change."

"Fair enough. I shall prepare a list. In the meantime, Campbell would like to meet with you and Abby in the conference room. She asked me to let her know when you'd arrived."

Uh-oh, that sounded serious. Grace held back a yawn. "I'll be ready in ten minutes." She walked to her desk and dumped her bag, regretting the fact she hadn't worked on the return flight from

London. She'd taken some time to review her emails yesterday, but somewhere in the middle of her overflowing inbox, she'd fallen asleep in front of her computer and woken up this morning with odd file folder wrinkles on the side of her face. Must've been the bike ride around London. There really wasn't any other explanation for her complete lack of energy.

She made a mental note to get more exercise and started by walking briskly to the law firm's kitchen, loading up the fancy espresso machine with her favorite brew, and willing the coffee to be extra strong. She'd thoroughly enjoyed her trip to London, but now that she was back she needed to refocus, starting by hammering out a mediation date with opposing counsel on the grocery cart case and scheduling a meeting with Hadley Construction, one of her major clients, about the regulatory enforcement letter they'd received while she was out. While the coffee was brewing, she set a reminder on her calendar to call Hadley's in-house counsel first thing in the morning.

The machine spurted and spewed the last drops into her cup, and Grace took a deep drink before making her way to the firm's conference room. Abby and Campbell were already there and they waved her over. As Grace approached, she spotted a box of donuts surrounded by an array of photos.

"Welcome back, stranger," Abby called out. "Pull up a donut. We're helping Campbell pick the decorations for the venue."

Wedding planning? Grace took a deep breath and swallowed a retort about how she had a ton of work to do and they were sitting around looking at decorations. "I think I'll pass on the donut because I just ate my way through London. And I'm happy to add my two cents to the wedding planning, but I can't stay long. Hadley is having a crisis over an EPA complaint that blew up while I was gone, and I need to spend some time today getting up to speed so I can be available for a lot of hand-holding."

Campbell pointed at the chair next to her. "Sit. I promise I didn't call this meeting for the sole purpose of showing you wedding ideas, although these ideas Roxanne sent over are amazing."

Grace reluctantly complied and forced her attention to the spread of photos. Campbell was right. The pictures displayed a fairy-tale scape, very romantic and very Campbell. Roxanne was Abby's girlfriend and she ran a successful wedding blog called the *Bride's Best Friend*. She and Abby had met last year while in the middle of a case for one of the firm's clients who owned a chain of wedding dress stores that had suddenly gone out of business. Roxanne had covered the story for her blog with the hope of spinning her success into a TV show about all things wedding. That particular venture hadn't worked out, but she now had a regular spot on a nationally syndicated morning show, and her blog was licensed worldwide. "These all look great, but this one," she tapped the photo in the middle, "this one is so you."

Campbell grinned. "That's my favorite. I love the way the light plays off of the silver ornaments. It'll look great in the photos."

Grace started to push away from the table. "Happy to help, but I really need to go. I have a lot of prep to do before tomorrow."

"About that," Campbell said. "I have a proposition for you."

Grace cast a glance at Abby to try to get a read for what Campbell was about to propose, but all she got was a smile. "Okay, spill."

"We're all busy, but you've got the biggest caseload right now."

Grace shook her head. "No offense, but I can't hand off any of these clients right now. They're all very high maintenance and if they think I'm not handling things personally, they'll go to another firm where they have a partner with a full team of doting associates dedicated to their happiness."

"Right," Abby said. "We get it. And with the regulatory issues along with the litigation, it basically means you have double the workload. What if we could bring someone on board to help you out even if it was just on a temporary basis?"

"That could be great, but I'd need to run the numbers and we'd have to talk about how that would look. I'm not sure we could get a really skilled attorney to take a temporary position for the money we could offer right now."

"What if I told you I'd already found someone?" Campbell said, looking at her watch. "In fact, she's probably waking up in my spare bedroom right about now."

"Wait, what?" Grace pushed through her foggy brain and wished she had another shot of espresso to bring clarity, but she had a feeling she knew exactly who Campbell was talking about. "Perry?"

"Yes. She would be perfect. I predict she's bored already and she can't leave the country until her passport comes in. She'll take a temporary position because she thinks she doesn't want to stick around, but in the meantime she could help you out and maybe, just maybe, she'll realize her life is better back here in the States. I know it's a big ask, but it would mean a lot to me if you could see your way clear to taking her on."

Grace let out a deep breath as she contemplated her options. Perry was smart—she'd graduated at the top of her class—but getting good grades didn't necessarily equate to being able to do the work and keep clients happy. But she had practiced law under some of the most adversarial conditions possible. Surely that would translate into being able to work with the Leightons and Hadleys of the world. And it wasn't like some other candidate was going to pop up out of nowhere. And Perry was in town with nothing else to do. If the few days they'd spent together in London was any indication, it was clear they were able to get along. She took another breath and made her decision. "Okay, let's do it."

Campbell clapped her hands and Grace hoped the celebration wasn't premature. What could go wrong?

❖

At noon on the dot, Campbell's doorbell rang, and Perry flung open the door and pulled her big brother, Justin, into a tight hug. "Man, it's good to see you."

Justin squeezed her hard. "You too, kiddo. I hear you've been getting into all kinds of trouble. Worldwide."

"Didn't Dad always say go big or go home?"

"Looks like you're doing some of each now," Justin said.

Perry started to correct him, to say Austin wasn't home anymore, but she didn't have the heart to break the mood. It was good to see him and hug him and hear his voice in person rather than via Skype. And after he'd worked so hard to be head of the household and keep their home after their parents died, she knew her words would hurt him to the core. Better to have this conversation after she confirmed her new assignment and already had a ticket to wherever in the world she was headed next. She pointed at the large duffle bag slung over his shoulder. "Are you moving into Campbell's place too?"

"You're hilarious." He shoved the bag toward her. "I brought you some clothes from the stash you left in your old room. I figured you might need them."

Perry peered inside at the clothes she'd stored at Justin's place when she'd left the country and smiled when she spotted her favorite RBG T-shirt on top. "You have no idea. I picked up a few shirts in London, but I'm running low when it comes to pants and stuff. Just for this, I'm going to buy your lunch, and as a bonus I'll tell you all about being rousted out of bed and escaping Crimea in a hidden compartment of a transport vehicle."

"I'm not entirely sure I want to know the details, but I'll take the broad strokes over good food. And I'm buying. Thai okay with you?"

She knew there was no sense arguing about who would pay. "Thai is perfect."

A few minutes later, they were in the car headed toward the UT campus. Justin scored a parking spot and they walked through the doors of Madam Mam's and Perry sniffed the air like a cartoon character dog following the scent of a nearby barbecue. "I love this place."

Justin laughed. "Don't I know it. You always picked it on your night to decide where we were going to eat. I thought you were going to turn into a curry." He started to walk to the hostess station but stopped and turned back toward her. He continued to the hostess stand, and when she asked how many in the party, he held up three fingers.

"What's up, Justin?" Perry asked, instantly curious. "You have someone special you want me to meet?"

"Not exactly," he said, looking over her shoulder with a half smile. She turned to follow his gaze and saw Campbell walking toward them. "I was hoping we could have a family lunch," he said. "You don't mind if Campbell joins us do you?"

She knew she shouldn't, but she did, mostly because it felt a bit like an ambush. If Campbell had been planning to join them, why hadn't she mentioned it before she left this morning? Of course, she'd slept through Campbell leaving. Maybe Campbell was being kind by letting her sleep in and she was reading way too much into her appearance here. If she was going to stay in Austin for any length of time, she needed to figure out a way to be okay with Campbell's micromanaging ways. "Of course it's okay," she said to Justin, mustering a half wave to Campbell to signal she was cool with it.

Campbell returned the wave and strode toward them. "I couldn't resist crashing when Justin mentioned you were coming here. I hope it's okay."

"Sure," Perry said. "The more the merrier. Although beware, I'll be performing a taste test on whatever you order. I'm starving and I haven't been here in forever."

After they were seated and had ordered enough food for a party twice their size, Perry decided to get the uncomfortableness out of the way. "I know you two think I'm still a kid you can fib to, but I figure there's a purpose behind this lunch besides making sure I get to enjoy some of the best Thai food outside of Thailand before I go back out into the world. Why don't you go ahead and tell me what it is before the food gets here?"

She watched Justin and Campbell exchange glances, like they were trying to decide who should speak first, and then Campbell cleared her throat. "It's true, I didn't show up today simply for the food. I have an opportunity I wanted to discuss with you, and I really hope you'll hear me out before you answer."

Perry's gut clenched at the word "opportunity" since it sounded like code for something she should probably rebel against. She flicked her eyes to Justin who was wearing his best, please try to make nice face and she channeled some of his calm demeanor. "Okay, let's hear it."

Campbell looked relieved at her response. "It's been almost a year since we started the firm and things are going really well. We're not quite ready to hire more permanent staff, but we do need some help to get us through a couple of labor-intensive cases." She paused. "Like first year associate kind of help."

Perry started to squirm in her chair, but she waited Campbell out rather than fire off a gut-level "no."

"I'm talking deposition prep, document review. It's grunt work, but it's important. We'll pay you well and there's an endless supply of good coffee and donuts. It may take a month for you to get your new passport and I figured this would be a decent way to kill the time."

Campbell had a point, but the idea of engaging in the kind of soul-crushing, mind-numbing tasks that most of her law school classmates were doing at big law firms all around the country made Perry nauseous, especially after she'd been on the front lines of major litigation in a foreign country—the kind that set precedent and changed lives. Campbell had a point though—she wasn't going to be able to do anything for the next month, and it wasn't like she was going to be happy sitting around waiting for the moment she could pick up her passport and get back to Lawyers For Change, but going from that level of responsibility to the role of an overpaid glorified clerk left her feeling hollow. "I don't know," she said, giving the most honest answer she could.

"I get it," Campbell said. "But you'd be doing us a big favor. Grace mostly."

Perry perked up at the mention of Grace's name. She'd wondered off and on since they'd parted at the airport how Grace was doing and whether she'd called the insanely tall blonde she'd been talking to on the plane in what would surely be a big mistake. "Why Grace?"

"She's got a couple of very demanding clients with pressing matters. She convinced them to come on board with us when she left her old firm, but they're used to the level of service they get from bigger firms and we need to show them we can shoulder the work seamlessly if she wants to keep them. They both have litigation ramping up right now, so we're going to have to hire someone to help out. I figured you'd be the perfect fit and you wouldn't mind since Grace flew all the way to London to help you with your passport."

Perry barely noticed the guilt trip. She did owe Grace a favor and they'd had a blast in London. The prospect of working directly with her was more enticing than doing grunt work in general, and for a brief moment, the image of Grace riding through the streets of London with her hair blowing in the breeze stirred decidedly unprofessional thoughts. Again.

"Look," Campbell said. "I know you don't want to do this, but—"

"I'll do it," Perry said, surprising herself and Campbell at the same time.

"Really?"

"Really, as long as everyone understands it's not permanent. I'm doing everything I can to get my new passport as quickly as possible, and as soon as it gets here, I'm going back to my real job."

Campbell sighed.

"I thought you'd be happy I said yes," Perry said, surprised Campbell wasn't celebrating the win.

Justin cleared his throat. "I think she was hoping you might stick around for the wedding."

Damn. She kept forgetting Campbell and her desire to be traditional. When she was in Crimea, she'd figured she could make a last-minute decision about attending the wedding, but now that she was here in Austin, she'd be a lame sister if she didn't stay. It felt like she was being trapped by the obligation, but she didn't want to be a total jerk about it. "Tell you what. I promise I'll be at the wedding. No matter what happens between now and then, but I'm not sure I can handle more than a month of pushing papers. Okay?"

"Okay."

She couldn't quite read Campbell's expression, but it looked like part relief and part frustration, but either way, it made her want to change the subject. "I met Wynne this morning. Granted, I wasn't very awake, but she seems cool."

Campbell smiled. "She is. I'm very lucky."

Perry grinned. "Yes, yes, you are." She arched out of Campbell's way as Campbell faux punched her while Justin laughed at the two of them tousling. She hated to admit it, but she'd missed them and the easy way they slipped back into family mode when they were together. Maybe sticking around for a month wouldn't be too much of a hardship, especially since she was going to be working with Grace.

CHAPTER EIGHT

Monday morning, Grace rolled over and slapped at the alarm clock without opening her eyes, but the buzzing wouldn't stop. She groaned and switched on the lamp beside her bed and stared at the clock, trying to figure out why her alarm was going off an hour before she'd set it. After a few fuzzy moments, she finally registered the sound was coming from her phone on the nearby dresser where she'd set it to keep her from hitting the snooze button repeatedly. She swung her feet out of bed and trudged across the room. She recognized the DC area code and answered the call. "One day you're going to get the time difference thing down."

Her comment was answered with a hearty laugh. "Probably not, but just think—while everyone else is sleeping, you can get a jump on the day. You'll thank me later."

"Sure, Dad. Whatever you say," Grace said as she wandered into the kitchen to start the coffee maker. "Is there a particular reason for this call other than to push me to be a better person?"

"Your mom and I will be in town next weekend and we'd like to have dinner with you. Make a reservation wherever you want and send the details to your mother."

"What if I have plans?"

"Like a date? If you're serious about her, bring her with you so we can meet her. If it's not serious, you can reschedule. We haven't seen you for a while."

Grace bit back a retort. She loved her father, but he was baiting her and she wasn't going to fall for it. There wasn't a date, but whether she confirmed or denied, she'd be giving up valuable, personal information. As a US senator, he'd willingly given up any pretense at a private life, and he seemed to think everyone else should do the same, but she wasn't interested in subjecting a date to dinner with the family unless she was announcing an engagement, and even then it would be a maybe. And she certainly didn't want to admit there were no dates of note on the horizon. "I'll make a reservation and text Mom."

"Perfect. Have a wonderful day!" He hung up before she could say good-bye and she recognized the move. Other people needed his attention and it was his duty to be there for them. Whatever. She could fill her parents in about the trip to London and how well the firm was doing at dinner.

She poured a cup of coffee, added cream, and curled into one of the barstools that lined the granite counter of her enormous, well-appointed kitchen. She should invite her parents over and break out the new set of All-Clad cookware Campbell had generously gifted her last month for her birthday, but hosting would prevent her from making a quick escape if the situation warranted. A few clicks on the phone later, she'd booked a reservation for three on Saturday night at Jeffrey's, purposely picking a place more to her taste than his. It wasn't a huge accomplishment, but checking the dinner reservation off her list did make her feel somewhat productive. Normally, she'd have a full workout in by now, but the whirlwind trip to England had thrown her sleep schedule into disarray. She made a mental note to look up tips for combating jet lag and idly wondered if Perry was suffering from the same issue.

Perry. She'd almost forgotten her agreement with Campbell. Perry was starting work this morning and if she didn't do some planning, Perry would be standing around looking for something to do. At her last firm Grace had a ready bank of eager law school interns and junior associates willing and ready to do anything she asked in order to impress the senior partners, but she doubted Perry was going to display the same level of enthusiasm for the type of mundane tasks she needed her to do. If Campbell's master plan was to get Perry to abandon traipsing around the world, working in dangerous places, boring wasn't going to cut it. Grace would need to let Perry have a glimpse of how exciting litigation could be, and to do that, she'd need to include her in some more substantial work. Doing so wasn't exactly going to lighten her own workload, but it would help Campbell out, and for that she was all in. Anything to take stress off her best friend in the run-up to the wedding.

An hour later, Grace walked into her office building, ready to tackle Mission Perry Clark. She was two steps in when she spotted a very dapper Perry engaged in banter with Graham, the office manager. A surprising development since Graham was usually very reserved with anyone he hadn't met before.

"Hey, Grace," Perry called out. "Come here and settle a friendly dispute, please."

She approached cautiously. "Hi, Perry. Good morning, Graham." She took a second to appraise Perry who'd shed her uniform of political T-shirts and cargo shorts in favor of tan chinos, a short sleeve white button-down, and a jade vest. "You look nice."

"Thanks. Figured I should play the part, at least on the first day."

Conscious she was still staring, Grace tore her gaze away. "What's this dispute I'm supposed to settle?"

"Graham here insists mead is making a comeback and I say no. Unless of course you're at a Renaissance faire and then feel free to put whatever you want in your tankard."

"You may have lost me at tankard," Grace said. "Give me a Holmegaard No. 5 any day of the week."

"A what?"

"It's a Danish glass, fire cut and polished by hand. Perfect for whiskey."

"Ah." Perry nodded. "A fancy-pants glass. I think I'll stick with my tankard if it's all the same to you. How about you, Graham?"

Grace stared him down, but the phone rang before he could answer, and he could not have looked more relieved to avoid the question. Grace turned back to Perry. "You ready to get started?" At Perry's nod, Grace led the way back to her office and motioned to one of the chairs in front of her desk. "I don't know what Campbell told you, but I have two important clients with looming matters. The first one is Leighton Industries and the other is Hadley Construction. Leighton is a product liability case, currently pending mediation, and if it doesn't settle, we're going straight to trial."

"What's the product?"

Grace paused for a second. "It's a grocery cart. I know, I know," she added at Perry's dubious look. "The plaintiff's case is crap, but she insists on going forward, and Leighton is unlikely to offer anything other than nuisance value."

"And the other case?"

"Hadley Construction was served last week with a regulatory action by the state version of the EPA, and I'm fairly certain an EPA case is coming. The allegation is illegal dumping."

Perry frowned. "Did they do it?"

"Did they engage in dumping? Yes. Was it illegal? That's another issue entirely."

"Seems like it should be pretty easy to determine."

Grace held back what she was sure would be perceived as a patronizing smile. "Tell you what. Why don't you look at the evidence and judge for yourself. Most of what we have on both cases is in electronic form and I've got an extra computer setup loaded with the documents. At my old firm, I'd probably have a team of interns and associates working the cases. We've tried some temporary help, but so far it's been kind of hit-and-miss and I could use a new set of eyes on the project."

"Temporary help of a different kind?"

Grace didn't take the bait. "You're smart, and while your experience isn't in traditional litigation, I figure it's given you the tools to problem solve—not a skill possessed by any of the contract attorneys we've encountered so far." She handed a flash drive to Perry. "All the pleadings to both cases are on there. Why don't you take the morning to review them, and then we can have lunch and talk strategy. Deal?"

Perry looked surprised at the assignment, which told Grace she'd taken the right tack. At a more traditional firm, the lead attorney on the case would normally tell the associate to start reviewing documents without necessarily providing much in the way of context and they generally wouldn't be seeking substantive input. While Grace didn't think she needed Perry's opinions about how the cases should be managed, Perry needed to feel like she was valued if she was going to be convinced to stick around.

"Sounds great. Where do you want me to set up?"

"I'll show you." Grace led the way out of her office and down the hall to the one spare office at the firm, outfitted with a basic desk, chair, computer, and boxes of files. "We've set this up as our war room. It's not fancy, but it's the best place for you to be to manage the litigation." She pointed at the boxes. "I know I said most of the discovery is electronic, but those are some older manuals, along with some key documents—company memos, etc. Don't worry about trying to sort it all out right now. The pleadings are your best bet for getting a handle on the case." She looked at her watch. "I've got a conference call in a few minutes. I'll check in later, okay?"

"Sure," Perry said, but she was already in the process of firing up the flash drive and flipping through the documents, so Grace left her to it. She'd barely made it back to her office when Abby burst through the door and settled into the chair Perry had occupied moments ago.

"How was London? What did you eat? What did you see? Any royal sightings? Tell me everything."

Grace grinned at Abby's infectious enthusiasm. She reached under her desk and produced a bottle of gin she'd purchased at Camden Lock. "I know this isn't your beverage of choice, but when in London…Besides, I rode a bicycle all over the city, breaking all kinds of traffic laws, in the acquisition of this fine spirit."

Abby raised her eyebrows. "You? On a bike? I'm trying to conjure up the image, but I'm having trouble getting there."

Grace chucked a paperclip at her. "I know you and Campbell think I'm a stick-in-the-mud, but I know how to have fun."

"And it sounds like you did. Any chance you got to share some of your fun with cute English girls?"

Grace flashed to riding alongside Perry, both of them laughing at their encounter with the angry Englishwoman and then to the way Perry stood close to her on the Eye in an effort to allay her fear of heights. She felt a flush of warmth at the memory, but when she caught Abby staring, she pushed the thoughts away, pledging to examine them later. "Sadly, no Englishwomen. But I did meet a woman on the plane. She's some kind of corporate raider and she lives here in Austin."

"Intriguing. When are you seeing her again?"

"When did you start running a dating service?" Grace deflected. Abby could be relentless when she got an idea in her head.

"You're hilarious," Abby said. "We could do a double date. Make that a triple date. Campbell wants to get together and discuss the wedding. What about this weekend?"

"Sure, Abby, let me bring a first date to a group discussion about weddings. What could possibly go wrong in that scenario? Besides, my parents are coming into town, and I'm having dinner with them on Saturday."

"Fine, but I want to hear more about this mysterious woman whose number you are hoarding away. Happy hour. Friday night." Abby pointed a finger at her. "You have until then to call her. Have lunch for your first date and then you can bring her out to meet us all for date number two. I predict a fall wedding."

Grace shooed her away. "I'll agree to happy hour with you, but nothing more. Now, beat it, I've got a call with Hadley in just a few."

Abby was barely out of sight before Graham buzzed through to remind her about her conference call with John Hadley, the CEO of Hadley Construction. Grace straightened the files on her desk, pulled a fresh notebook from one of the drawers, and fished in her purse for her favorite pen. When she pulled it out, Danika's card was stuck on the clip—a coincidence Abby would've said was a sign. She set the card on her desk and stared at it. Danika was pretty and accomplished and flirty, and she had no idea why she was hesitant about calling her. Sure, she was busy with work, but the few relaxing days she'd spent in London were a sign she could do with a lot more fun in her life. She propped the card up against her phone and pledged to make the call as soon as she was off the phone with Hadley.

Perry leaned back in her chair and yawned. She'd spent the morning reviewing the pleadings in both cases and was finishing up with some key documents the Hadley Construction company had emailed over that morning. From what she'd seen so far, she was convinced Grace's client deserved whatever they had coming. In fact, she was surprised the EPA hadn't yet found a way to get a piece of this case. The only question she had after reviewing all of the evidence was why Grace was wasting her time on a loser of a client who'd clearly engaged in illegal dumping with no regard for the law or the environment.

"Are you ready for a break?"

Perry turned to see Grace framed in the doorway, looking very corporate in her dark navy suit. Perry liked the more casual look Grace had sported in London better, but she had to admit the stark lines of the suit gave off an authoritative vibe that was strangely alluring. "Uh, sure." She signed out of the discovery database and followed Grace toward the lobby, waving at Graham as they left.

"This is me," Grace said, pointing at the Nissan Armada.

"Wow."

"I can't tell if that's a good 'wow' or a bad one."

Perry slowly walked the perimeter of the monster vehicle. "It's an 'I didn't know you had a family of six that you need to transport around town' kind of wow."

"Very funny." Grace clicked the remote. "Get in. I'm starving."

Perry opened the passenger door, grabbed onto the roofline, and hauled herself up into the massive SUV. Once she'd settled into the cushioned leather seat, she surveyed the interior that more closely resembled the interior of a jet airliner than a car.

"Quit acting like you've never been in a car before."

"It's just a lot. Most of the vehicles in Crimea were stripped down pieces of crap. This is pretty luxurious."

"You say that like it's a bad thing."

"It's whatever." Perry shrugged. She wanted to say that no one needed a vehicle this decadent when the cost of a car like this could feed a village, but she used the same analogy with her before and she didn't want to pick a fight with Grace on her first day working at the office. "It's definitely a sweet ride," she conceded, hoping Grace wouldn't press her to be more specific about her opinion. "What's for lunch?" she asked to change the subject.

"I'm craving Tex-Mex. Sound good to you?" Grace asked as she pulled out of the parking lot.

"Absolutely."

"Guero's has plenty of vegetarian choices if that works for you."

Perry was touched by Grace's consideration. "Sounds great to me, but you don't have to do that."

"Do what?"

"Tailor your restaurant choices around my diet. I can usually find something to eat anywhere. I've gotten pretty good at being creative with whatever ingredients a restaurant has on hand."

"When did you decide to become a vegetarian?" Grace asked. "I mean, I have vivid memories of you trying to steal food off my plate when I'd eat with you and Campbell back in the day, and you were definitely a carnivore then."

"True," Perry laughed as she recalled a specific memory. "Remember that time Dad burned all the hamburgers but one and you got it because you were the guest. I think I broke a tooth on mine."

"Yes," Grace said. "He wasn't so great with the grill, but he was as polite as they come."

"He was." Perry turned her head toward the passenger side window and closed her eyes to spend a moment reliving the sight of her dad in his Kiss the Chef apron standing near the grill. She could hear her mother calling out to remind him to keep the charcoal from flaring up, but he was usually in the middle of recounting a great story he'd heard or listening intently while they relayed some stories about their own exploits. Inevitably, the meat would catch on fire, not to be noticed until the smell of burning food wafted through the air. Her mom would appear in the doorway of the patio to warn him again, but by that time the flames would've engulfed the food, charbroiling it beyond recognition. Her dad would laugh and good-naturedly bite into his hamburger, declaring well done to be the perfect temperature.

She shook away the sweet and sour memory and forced her focus back to the present. Grace had asked her a question. Something about food. What was it?

"Are you okay?"

She met Grace's eyes and saw the same solace she'd offered when they were riding the Eye back in London. "Sure. Memories. You know."

"I get it. Sorry."

"Not your fault. Pretty sure I brought it up." She fished around for a change in subject. "How are your parents?"

"They're okay. Splitting time between here and DC. Mom's not a fan of the back and forth, but I think Dad loves it. Man of the people and all. They're coming in this weekend and I haven't seen them for a while, so that'll be nice."

Perry heard a slight edge and Grace didn't make eye contact, like she was both anticipating and slightly dreading the reunion. "I always liked your dad."

"Everyone did. Does. Which is good if you want to be in politics."

"But maybe not as good if you're the daughter in the background…"

Grace flinched slightly at Perry's words.

"Sorry," Perry said. "I have no filter. It can be a problem."

"It's okay. You're right. I mean, I can't really complain, my parents always made sure I had everything I ever needed and more, but there were definitely days when I would've preferred to have them to myself instead of sharing them with the entire state of Texas." Grace backed into a space in front of Guero's and shut off the engine. "Ignore my rambling. I know I should be lucky to have parents at all."

Something about her tone tugged at Perry and she reached over and clasped Grace's hand. "Please. I get it. And you're allowed to have your folks and have feelings about your relationship with them. You don't have to be perfect all the time, you know."

"Ha! Very funny." Grace pulled the keys out of the ignition and dangled them in the air. "Come on, I'm starving."

A few minutes later, they were drinking iced tea and stuffing their faces with chips and salsa. Perry loved the abandon with which Grace enjoyed her food, mostly because it was so at odds with the rest of her tightly laced demeanor. Watching Grace savor all the taste sensations led her to wonder what other things Grace savored and did she throw herself so completely into other pursuits?

"Are you going to eat that?"

"What?" Perry shook from her reverie and followed the line of Grace's hand. Her slender, elegant hand with long, beautiful fingers, pointing at the last chip in the basket. "Chip, right. No, help yourself."

Their server showed up just then and Perry was grateful for the distraction of ordering. Like it had in London, her childhood crush had come roaring back, and she needed to get a grip. Grace was her boss now. Kind of. No, not kind of—for real. But that wasn't the only reason her feelings felt so misplaced. They lived in completely different worlds and enjoyed completely different lifestyles. Grace was ultra-professional, representing corporations, while she preferred to rough it out in the real world, protecting the rights of the little guy. If they had online dating profiles, no algorithm in the world would match them up, and all the tingly sensations she felt when Grace was in the room were nothing more than the residual angst of youth.

Once the waiter left, Grace got down to business. "Tell me your first impressions about the cases."

Perry hesitated. "Are you sure?"

"Absolutely."

"Okay. Let's talk grocery carts first. Leighton Industries will probably win at trial, but I think they should settle with the plaintiff."

"Interesting conclusion."

"I understand the words you're saying, but your tone is all she's crazy for thinking that."

"Got me," Grace said. "What's the point of settling if they have a slam dunk case?"

"To do the right thing. I mean yes, Annie does seem to be exaggerating her injuries, but clearly she's in pain. Who would go to the trouble of having a nerve stimulator implanted in her body if she wasn't experiencing serious issues?"

"No offense, but that's a little naive. People do all kinds of crazy things when there's a big payout on the horizon."

"Why is it whenever anyone says 'no offense,' they are absolutely about to offend?" Perry asked, trying not to be too pissed off at Grace's condescending tone.

"You have to admit I have seen a few more of these cases than you."

"True. But I bet Leighton will spend more to try this case than they could to settle."

"Now you're trying to run me out of a job."

Perry stared at Grace's narrowed eyes, trying to determine if she was serious.

"Quit looking at me like that. I'm only kidding. If I thought settling was the right thing to do, that's what I'd advise Leighton to do. But there's an intangible cost to settling. Giving in on this case makes them a target for other lawsuits. A show of strength can be a healthy dose of prevention."

"Okay."

"I can tell you disagree."

Perry didn't want to have this argument. It wasn't like her to back down from a debate, but this wasn't her war to win. Working these cases was nothing more than a few skirmishes on the path back to her work with Lawyers for Change, so keeping the peace was the best choice of action to just get through it, and she shoved aside the internal voice that said she'd argue more if someone other than Grace were on the other side. She settled on a vague, "Give me some time to see your point."

Grace eyed her carefully, like she was sure Perry was saving ammo for another battle, but she pressed on. "Any thoughts about the other case?"

"How can I say this tactfully? Hadley Construction is a bad corporate citizen."

Grace laughed. "Don't hold anything back." She stared at Perry as if wondering why she wasn't laughing too. "Wait a minute. You really think that?"

"Of course, I do," Perry said, not bothering to hide her indignation. "They're engaged in illegal dumping without any regard to the environment or the people who own the land around them."

"Well, that's not entirely true."

Perry held up her hand and ticked off the facts she'd summarized in her notes. "One, they accumulated an illegal amount of waste. Two, they hid it from the regulators. Three, they may have offered to remediate, but only after they were caught." She put her hand down. "I could go on, but what's the point? Have *they* offered to settle or do they not want to set a bad precedent either?"

"Slow your roll, kiddo. It's not as simple as that. First off, they had a plan to recycle the waste which is why they kept it in the first place. On their own land, I might add. Second, the only reason they got caught was because the busybody farmer next door illegally flew a drone over their property. Third, if the state was reasonable, yes, this whole case would be resolved out of court, but in my experience this agency doesn't leave much room for compromise."

Perry heard everything she said, but it was all colored by the word "kiddo," and she could not even. She wasn't a kid. She was a grown woman with a law degree just like Grace and Campbell and Abby, and her age didn't make her opinion any less valid. "So, I guess they'll pay, just not the right people."

Grace scowled. "What's that supposed to mean?" She held up a hand. "Never mind, I'm pretty sure I know, and I resent the implication we'd drag out the case to earn a fee. Is that the kind of lawyer you think I am?"

Perry wanted to say no, but the truth was she didn't know anything about Grace's practice at the firm other than she represented corporate clients over the little guy. She studied Grace's face for a moment and detected a trace of hurt behind the frown. She'd either hit a sore spot or landed a punch that wasn't warranted, and the fact that she'd known Grace for most of her life meant she should give her the benefit of the doubt. "Sorry, I get a little heated sometimes. To be perfectly honest, I don't know much about the firm, other than the story about how you, Campbell, and Abby all quit your high-paying, big law jobs to go into business for yourselves. Campbell doesn't talk shop much with me. Care to give me the inside scoop?"

The frown disappeared and Grace's shoulders relaxed. "Sure. We have three simple principles. We're client-focused which means we tailor our work for each individual client—nothing cookie-cutter. We're efficient—no wasting time pursuing strategies that aren't agreed to in advance. And we're accountable—unlike firms where associates do all the work and the partners take the credit, we work on the cases ourselves. And when it comes to fees, we're creative and we work with our clients to find a solution that meets both of our needs. Some clients want the traditional retainer and regular billing, but a lot prefer flat fees so they know up front what their obligations are going to be. Sometimes that works out well for us, and sometimes we get burned when a case turns out to be more complicated than we expected and takes longer to resolve."

"But if it's easier, do you give back the money?"

"No. Are you going to tell me you think we're crooks if we don't?"

Perry squirmed in her seat. "I wasn't, but it's a valid point, don't you think?"

"It's worth raising, but here's the deal. In exchange for the security of knowing their final costs going in, the client takes a gamble that they may get a deal on a complex case just like we take a gamble that we won't wind up getting paid pennies on the dollar for our usual hourly rate by accepting a flat fee up front. We all have something at risk."

She had a point, and Perry had to admit she had no experience with fee arrangements at all since she'd only ever worked for nonprofits representing people for free, using funds that had been donated for the cause. "How do you decide whether to agree to a flat fee versus hourly billing?"

"Experience mostly. Between the three of us, we've worked all kinds of cases and have a pretty good handle on what's involved and when outcomes are predictable and when they aren't. And sometimes, it boils down to the client's comfort level."

"Is Hadley a flat fee client?"

"Up until last year, Hadley had only worked with big firms, the last one being my old firm, who he believed took advantage of his lack of experience to milk his litigation for every dime they could. He came to us because he heard we employ creative approaches, tailored to each client we represent." Grace shook a chip in her direction. "Which is where you come in. I want you to look at out of the box ways to represent Hadley Construction. Our goal is to get the case tossed out before it even gets set for trial, but if we're forced to go forward, let's find a way to reverse the first impression and show they're indeed good corporate citizens who made an honest mistake. Do you think you can suppress your innate disdain for the company and apply your creative legal mind to the task at hand?"

Perry examined Grace's words, searching for a sign Grace was messing with her, but her plea seemed sincere. Principles aside, she wasn't sure she would ever be able to resist a request from Grace. Besides, it wasn't like she was agreeing to add corporate defender to her résumé. This work was temporary and targeted, with the added bonus of allowing her to work closely with Grace. She looked into Grace's eyes, and the earnest expression reflected there was the tipping point. She could do this one thing without fear of losing her integrity in the process. Right?

Chapter Nine

Grace read the short and sweet text from Abby and laughed. *Birdie's. Now. Put down the files and get your butt here.* She surveyed the contents of her desk. It would take hours to plow through the rest of the work she'd had planned for the day, and it was already six o'clock on Friday night. Since she was doomed to work on Saturday anyway, she might as well join the gang for happy hour and start fresh in the morning.

The office building was quiet as everyone else had already left for the day. Grace liked staying after hours, often getting her best work done in the absence of ringing phones and visiting clients, and as much as she enjoyed the camaraderie with Abby and Campbell, the quiet of the evening allowed her to focus. She walked through, making sure the lights were off, noticing a noise that sounded like the copier was running. She eased up to the war room and spied Perry standing in front of the copier but staring at a piece of paper in her hand and grinning like she'd found a long lost treasure map.

"You look way too happy for someone working on a Friday night," Grace said.

Perry jumped. "Holy shit, Grace. You scared the crap out of me."

"What're you doing? Do you know what time it is?"

Perry shook her head. "Not really. I got a little lost in all of this." She spread her hands to indicate the files piled on the table.

"I found some good stuff. You want to sit down and I can walk you through it?"

"No."

"No?"

"I mean, yes, I want you to walk me through it, but not here. Grab your stuff." She rolled her arm to signal Perry to hurry. "Come on, let's go out."

"Really?"

Grace heard the hint of suggestion in Perry's tone and realized her mistake right away. She rushed to correct the misimpression. "I meant we have a firm meeting to get to."

Perry held her gaze for a moment before her eyes dropped to the file in her hand. "You know, since I'm not actually part of the firm, I'm good. I think I'll stick around here and work a while longer."

Grace reached over and grabbed the file. "Partner privilege. You're done for the night. This meeting is really important. Come on."

Perry finally acquiesced and followed her out of the office to the Armada. She watched while Perry made a big show about how much effort it took to climb inside. "You should quit making fun of me. This car is extremely safe and handles like a champ."

"This car is a gas guzzler and safety is relative. I bet you could run over a family of four and never even feel it. If you don't tip over first."

Grace laughed. "Were you always this uptight?"

"Me?"

"Yes, you. I have fond memories of a rough-and-tumble kid who was completely fearless. Now you're sitting there talking about safety like a little old lady. It's like you're twenty-five, going on eighty."

"Again, I ask, me? Because you're the most conservative person I know."

"I hope you mean conservative with a little c, not a big one, because that particular C word is a fighting word." She waited for

Perry's nod. "Yes, when it comes to finances and the rest of the firm operation, I'm careful and steady, but that doesn't mean I'm not fun. Whose idea was it to ride through the streets of London in pursuit of gin?"

"You have a point. Where is this meeting we're headed to?"

Grace turned the car into the parking lot at Birdie's. "More evidence that I can be fun. It's Friday and we're here for happy hour. Drinks on the firm, because Abby had a big win in a case today which you would know if you'd emerged from the war room at any point."

She locked arms with Perry and led her into the bar where Abby, Roxanne, Wynne, and Campbell were already seated around a large table. "Look who I found holed up in the back room. This kid needs a drink." She felt Perry flinch slightly, but when she met her eyes, she couldn't read her expression. Disappointment, maybe? As fast as she saw the emotion, it was gone. "What's your pleasure?"

"I'll have whatever you're having, but I'll get it. You go sit down."

"Manhattan with Bulleit. There should be a tab going."

Grace watched as Perry sauntered to the bar. Perry was only a few feet away before Grace noticed she wasn't the only one watching. At least half a dozen other women in the bar had their eyes on Perry's trim figure as she cut through the crowd, and Grace wanted to shout at them all to quit ogling her best friend's little sister. She didn't though, mostly because she had a feeling her desire to shout was about something other than being protective, a feeling she quickly buried.

Perry edged her way through the crowd toward the bar, smiling at several women along the way who'd clearly noticed she was new to this bar scene. The bartender was a broad-shouldered brunette with close-cropped hair who crossed her arms and looked down on her with a stern expression. "ID," she said.

"What if all I want is soda with lime?" Perry asked.

"Is that all you want?"

"Uh, no." Perry instinctively reached for her wallet before she remembered her only ID was her temporary passport and it was sitting on the dresser in the guest room at Campbell's place. She made a mental note to get a new driver's license.

"It's okay, Birdie, she's with me."

Perry looked over her shoulder to find Campbell standing behind her. "Look, it's Campbell to the rescue. Again." She turned back to Birdie and placed an order for two Manhattans.

"Since when do you drink Manhattans?" Campbell asked.

"Since when did you start monitoring my choice of beverage?" Birdie showed up right then with the Manhattans in thick, substantial whiskey glasses Perry knew Grace would appreciate. She reached into her pocket, but Campbell put a hand on her arm.

"I got it. We have a tab."

Perry pulled out some bills. "Fine, but do I have your permission to tip the bartender?"

Campbell frowned. "What's up with you? And what's up with the rescue and permission remarks?"

Perry took the drinks from Birdie who nodded in appreciation of the large tip and jerked her chin at an open spot a few feet away. Perry set the drinks down on the table and faced Campbell. "I didn't realize I was coming to happy hour."

"Perry, you're not making any sense. What are you trying to say?"

She started to answer but stopped when she realized Campbell was right. She wasn't making any sense, and she took a minute to boil down her feelings. It was bad enough being carded at the bar, but having to be rescued by your big sister when you were trying to buy drinks for your junior high crush was an unfair add-on. And to top it all off, she wouldn't even be in Austin if Campbell hadn't sent Grace on Mission Rescue Perry and persuade her to come home. With the added pressure to stick around for the wedding, it felt like the walls were closing in. She wanted to snap at Campbell, but the impulse felt self-indulgent.

"Grace kind of roped me into coming out tonight," Perry said. "She said we were going to a meeting. If I'd known you were all just hanging out, I probably would've stayed at the office or gone home to catch up on some reading."

"Hello, who are you? So, now you're not only against corporations, you're against the idea of burning off a little steam after a hard week's work? Abby had a big win today and we're here to raise a glass. We were trying to include you. Would it kill you to act like you enjoy our company for a little while?"

Perry knew she was being a jerk, but her instinct was to dig in. She counted out a few silent seconds to adjust her mindset. Campbell was right. They had every right to celebrate a win, even if it probably meant the little guy had gotten screwed over in favor of Abby's client. And she had no idea why she suddenly felt like she was coming out of her skin, but the desire to run was persistent and urgent. She focused her energy on resisting the impulse. "Sorry. I haven't had to be social in a while, so I'm rusty. I should get Grace's drink to her before the ice melts." She picked up the glasses and started to walk back toward their table. She was only a few steps in when she froze at the sight of the woman from the plane. The one who'd flirted mercilessly with Grace, and who was in the process of a redo at the very table where they were headed, and Perry barely resisted the desire to hurl the contents of her glass at the interloper.

"So, what's she like?" Abby asked.

"I decided not to call her, so let it go, Abby."

"Call her?" Abby frowned. "Who are you talking about?"

"Danika. Who are you talking about?" Grace asked.

"Perry. Campbell's little sister, but if you'd like to talk about the mysterious woman you met on the plane, feel free to dish."

"Abby, leave her be." Roxanne placed a hand on Abby's arm.

"It's okay, Roxanne," Grace said. "Danika is not mysterious. She's just a person and she lives in Austin. I called her and left a message earlier today, but I haven't heard back."

"Welcome to the twenty-first century, Grace," Abby said. "Not everyone checks their voice mail." She pointed at Grace's phone lying on the table. "You should text her and invite her to join us."

"We've had this conversation. And I'm not going to become a text-stalker. She's a grown-up woman with lots of responsibilities. I'm sure she'll check her phone messages at some point. I'm not in any hurry."

"Speaking of grown-up women, how's it working with the exact opposite?" Abby asked. "Perry giving you any trouble?"

Grace instinctively glanced across the room where Perry stood at the bar talking to Campbell. There was a time she wouldn't have been able to imagine Perry as anything but a skinny, insecure tomboy, but now she was a striking young woman who commanded the space she occupied with sass and confidence. Her lack of convention in dress, in career choice, in the spiky way she wore her hair, might cause most people to write her off as just a kid, but Grace suspected there was a lot more maturity there than anyone suspected. She looked back at Abby. "She's plenty grown-up."

"Okay," Abby said, stringing out the word, "but I asked if you liked working with her."

Grace focused on ignoring Abby's intense stare. "Perry. Sure. It's okay."

"It's kind of weird seeing her looking all adult. Last time I saw her was at our graduation and she still looked like a little kid."

Grace fished around for a memory of that day. Her parents had both been in attendance not only to support her, but because her father had been asked to give the commencement address. She was used to his presence drawing most of the attention in the room, but on that day in particular—her special day—all the focus on him had rubbed her the wrong way. She'd left the room right after the ceremony ended to get some air and ran into Perry who was standing outside, looking like she was headed to a dive bar.

"Aren't you supposed to be inside celebrating?" Perry asked. Grace sighed. "It's a little stuffy in there."

"Word. I mean if you plan on ruling the world, there's a lot of inspiration but not much for people who just want to do their small part to make it a better place. All those new lawyers fawning over your dad and I bet most of them barely heard a word he said."

Grace reflected on the content of her father's speech. Like most of his speeches, it was inspiring, and he'd issued a call for her classmates to use their new skills and apply them to public service, to help those less fortunate. She agreed with the charitable sentiment, but after three years of hard work, she was ready to enjoy the spoils of her success. Like most of the top ten percent of her class, she was going to a top-tier firm, but it was clear from Perry's tone, they didn't share an opinion on the definition of success. "Is there something wrong with wanting to rule the world?"

Perry kicked at a pebble with the toe of her sneaker. "Other than the fact that by definition, not everyone can do it? It's a zero-sum game. There are like four hundred new lawyers in that room. You think there's room at the top for all of them? The scramble to the top will be like crabs in a bucket—most people are going to get crushed under the weight of other people's desires. Why not redefine success and help each other out instead of using other people as stepping-stones to get to the top?"

"Because someone has to be in charge, to lead." Grace felt the tinny inauthenticity of her response even as she spoke the words, but she pressed on. "Otherwise, we just have chaos and anarchy."

Perry shrugged like she didn't care, but the expression in her eyes was sympathetic, like she saw something in Grace that Grace couldn't possibly see. "If you say so."

"What's that supposed to mean?" The sympathy and the brush-off got under Grace's skin.

Perry smiled. "Don't mind me. I'm just doing my usual bit of challenging the patriarchy." She linked arms with Grace. "You should get back in there and celebrate."

She led the way back into the hall and Grace followed, full of more questions than answers.

"She's always been a bit wiser than the rest of us. I think losing their parents when she was so young affected her even more than it did Campbell and Justin. Don't get me wrong, they were both great role models, but I think Perry felt she had to find her own way." She reflected on Perry's sense of style, her rebellious nature. "And she has."

"She's definitely taken on more weighty cases than I had at her age," Wynne said. "That journalist in Crimea she was representing was facing hard time simply for writing a blog."

"I'm thinking his blog wasn't about weddings," Roxanne said, prompting a bout of laughter from the group.

Grace lifted her water glass and took a sip of her drink. She'd been working so hard lately, this respite was a nice change of scene and there was no better group of people to unwind with than these women.

"Don't look now," Abby said, shoving her in the arm. "But that woman over there is checking you out."

"You realize that saying 'don't look now' only makes a person want to look, right?"

"Don't be that person. She's headed this way. Tall, blonde, Abba meets Charlize Theron."

Could it be? Grace ignored Abby's admonition and turned in her seat just in time to catch Danika smiling at her as she stepped closer. She returned the smile, hesitantly at first, but then she glanced over at the bar and saw Perry engaged in conversation with Campbell, apparently unaware the Swede had made an appearance, and she smiled with more confidence.

"Hello, Manhattan, nice to see you on the ground this time," Danika said.

Grace stood to avoid feeling like Danika was towering over her, and Perry's words about power flooded back into her mind until she brushed them away. This wasn't that. "Hello, Margarita, nice to see you too."

Danika leaned in close. "I hope it's okay for me to come over here. I promise I'm not stalking you. I was here after work and was going to call you later, but then I was pleasantly surprised to find you here."

Normally, Grace would've preferred to set the terms of her next meeting with a potential date, but Grace decided the distraction of Danika's presence would do her some good, although she wasn't entirely sure why she needed to be distracted right now. "I'm glad you did. Have a seat and meet my friends."

She motioned for Danika to take the spot next to her. The one Perry had occupied. She glanced over at the bar as Danika settled into the chair and saw Perry staring directly at her, her eyes narrowed. Grace wasn't entirely sure what to make of her expression, but she knew Perry wasn't happy and she knew she cared about that more than she should. In an effort to keep from letting it bother her, she dove into conversation with Danika and introduced her to Abby, Roxanne, and Wynne.

"All lawyers?" Danika asked.

"Almost." Grace pointed at Roxanne. "Roxanne here is the Bride's Best Friend."

Danika lit up. "Wow, really? My brother is a huge fan."

"Your brother?" Grace asked.

"Not a traditional bride, I know, but still planning a wedding to his boyfriend, and he thinks Roxanne has the best advice on the planet."

Roxanne smiled. "Best compliment ever, and I'm making a mental note to do a column devoted to an all-male wedding party."

"He'll love that, and he'll be so excited that we met." Danika turned to Wynne. "And you're a lawyer?"

"I am, and I'm about to be a bride. I'm marrying that one's law partner." Wynne pointed to Grace. "So we're one big happy family."

"It's true," Grace replied. "Now, it's your turn. Tell us about you. I only know that you like tequila and that you travel internationally for business."

"I'm in corporate mergers and acquisitions for a local venture capital firm. We do a lot of work in Europe and Asia, and the international trade is a definite perk, but I travel so frequently, I often feel out of touch when I'm back home."

"I'd love to travel," Wynne said, "but I haven't had much of a chance. What's the best place you've ever been?"

Danika started to answer when Perry and Campbell reappeared at the table. Grace noticed Perry glaring in Danika's direction and instinctively stood. "Sorry I stole your seat."

"You didn't," Perry said with a pointed look at Danika's back. "Please sit. I'm good."

Wynne patted the chair next to her that Campbell had occupied and waved Perry over. "Come sit by me. I'd love to spend more time with my future sister-in-law while I can."

Perry eased into the seat next to Wynne. "You remember Perry," Grace said to Danika. "She was with me on the flight from London."

"I do. Hi, Perry," Danika said with a broad smile.

"Danika was about to tell us her favorite place to travel," Abby chimed in. "Apparently, she's a world traveler like you."

"Really?" Perry placed her elbows on the table and leaned forward. "Do tell, what is your favorite place in all the world?"

Grace winced at the obvious sarcasm in Perry's tone, but Danika answered easily as if she didn't notice the friction.

"It's a hard question. There's hot climate and cold ones and both have their allure. If I absolutely had to choose my favorite place it would be Paris. The food, the fashion, the people. So much to love."

Everyone at the table murmured their appreciation. Everyone but Perry whose head shake was almost imperceptible. Grace saw it though and Perry caught her watching. Grace couldn't resist. "Perry, what's your favorite place to travel?"

"Well, considering I've rarely traveled for pleasure, it's not a fair comparison. Most of the places I go are either desolate, war-torn, or dominated by an authoritarian regime, but I did have a fantastic time in London last week. The Eye, Camden Market, and the gin bicycle tour with an excellent travel companion. Couldn't ask for better than that." She finished her statement with a pointed look in Danika's direction. Grace looked between them and was certain she detected an edge beneath their smiles. Why did it suddenly feel like these two women were engaged in an epic battle and she was smack in the middle of the battlefield?

Chapter Ten

Perry wandered into the kitchen in boxers and a tank top and tugged open the fridge. The best thing about Wynne being around was she could be sure the kitchen was well-stocked. Left to her own devices, Campbell would order takeout every night of the week. Perry reached for the orange juice, some vegetables, and the tofu Wynne had picked up on her last trip to the store. She took her time chopping mushrooms, peppers, onions, and garlic, and then sautéed the mixture in a dab of oil while she pressed and seasoned the tofu. Within a few minutes, the entire kitchen smelled like heaven. She turned down the heat, added the tofu, and scrambled the ingredients in the pan.

"OMG, that smells amazing." Wynne walked by her and went straight to the burr grinder. "I'll make you coffee if I can have a bite."

Perry grinned. "You don't have to make me coffee, but that would be fantastic. I take it black. And you can have a whole plate of this scramble. I made plenty to share."

"Did I hear the word share in conjunction with whatever smells amazing in this almost virgin kitchen?" Campbell strode into the room. "I see Wynne beat me to the coffee offer, but I'll gladly outbid her if there's only enough food for one."

Perry pointed at the table. "Set the table, it's almost ready."

Campbell and Wynne moved effortlessly around each other as they gathered plates and silverware, and as Perry watched their dance, she realized her career-driven sister had changed. For most of her life, Campbell's focus had been squarely directed at helping Justin keep their tiny family intact and becoming a successful lawyer, but it was pretty clear her priorities had shifted to include her relationship with Wynne, and Perry could tell Campbell was well and truly love-struck. "You guys are cute together."

Campbell grinned and slipped her arm around Wynne's waist. "We kind of are, aren't we?"

"It doesn't count when you say it, but yes," Perry said. "You are. Well, mostly Wynne."

"I'd protest, but you're right. Wynne is definitely the better half." Campbell set the last plate on the table. "You could have wedded bliss too, you know."

"Ha. Very funny." Perry scooped the contents of the skillet into a large serving bowl and handed it to her. "You have bride-to-be syndrome."

"What's that supposed to mean?"

"You're all into the dress and the flowers and the cake and the romancey stuff, and it goes to your head. You start thinking the whole world should feel like this, therefore, you think you can sprinkle some of your happily ever after dust on everyone you see and make the world a happy place."

Wynne laughed. "True. All true."

Campbell clutched her chest. "Et tu, Wynne?"

Perry rolled her eyes with a cynicism she didn't feel. At least not toward Campbell and Wynne. After a week with them, she was convinced the love they felt for each other was the real deal, and it reminded her of another relationship that was gone too soon. "I wish Mom and Dad could be here for your wedding. They would've loved all the mushy stuff."

Campbell walked toward her and hugged her close. "They would've wouldn't they?"

"Absolutely. And they would've loved you, Wynne." She poked Campbell on the shoulder. "Wynne grounds you."

Campbell's smile was big and bright. "She does, and I like it." Her eyes lit up. "Just you wait. One day, you're going to meet someone who steals your heart and makes you want to stay in one place for longer than a hot minute."

Perry twitched at the suggestion. "Not going to happen. I'm a nomad, sis. Traveling the world. I don't have time to be tied down. I'm a no strings attached kind of girl." She glanced at Wynne. "No offense."

Wynne gave her a "who me" look. "The string is not offended."

"You say that now," Campbell said. "But love will strike you when you least expect it. Look at Grace. Talk about career focused, but she travels all the way to London only to meet an amazing woman from Austin on the plane. What are the odds?"

Perry's stomach churned at the mention of Danika, but she forced a smile. "Yeah, I don't think they're the perfect match you think they are."

"I don't know about that. What's your theory?"

"They hardly know each other. Hello, I was on the plane. If there was a love connection, I would've noticed."

"Is that why you were such a jerk to Danika last night?"

"I wasn't a jerk." Perry looked everywhere but at Campbell as she delivered the remark since Campbell had a near perfect lie-meter. She kind of had been a jerk, but only because she couldn't stand to see Grace fawning all over the tall, over-confident blonde like she was God's gift to lesbians. Surely Grace could see Danika was a big, flirty faker who was likely to draw Grace in and then ditch her for the next gorgeous woman she met on a plane to London or, God forbid, Paris. The problem was that Grace was so focused on her work, she seemed willing to accept the first treat offered when she came up for air. *And what did you do? You acted like a bratty kid.*

Ugh. Perry shook her head. She had no business giving relationship advice since she had no desire to be in one herself, but Grace was gorgeous and accomplished and smart, and she deserved the kind of relationship Campbell had with Wynne and

Abby had with Roxanne. Maybe she wasn't an expert, but she still thought Grace would be better off holding out for the real deal.

"That was delicious," Campbell said, pushing her plate away. "If you're going to stay here, I'm going to get fat, fast."

"No worries, sis. Believe it or not, this was a pretty low-cal breakfast, and I won't be here too much longer."

"That's not what I meant. You know you're welcome to stay as long as you want, but if you ultimately decide to stay in Austin, you might want your own place."

Perry knew what was happening. For however long she stayed, Campbell would circle around the issue of her making the move to Austin permanent. Perry's first instinct was to cut that thinking short, but there really wasn't any sense continually reminding Campbell she was going to get on a plane as soon as her new passport came in. Besides, as far as places to hang out went, Campbell's house was the perfect stopover. Great kitchen, comfortable bed, and a fairly easy job to rake in some cash until she moved on to the next thing.

And she got to work with Grace. Total bonus, even if she was helping some money-grubbing capitalists hell-bent on making a buck over saving the environment and making plaintiffs whole. "Yeah, maybe. We'll see."

"Wynne and I are meeting with Roxanne today to go over some details about the wedding. Want to come with?"

Perry scrunched her face. "Not really my jam, but if you're riding together, can I borrow your car? I have a few errands to run and I haven't really had time since you put me right to work."

"I thought you didn't have your license."

"It's not like it was suspended or anything. Besides, I went online last night and reported it lost. DPS emailed me a temporary card until the new one comes in. If it takes a while, you may need to mail it to me."

Campbell exchanged a look with Wynne. "Yeah, okay." She pointed to the wall by the door to the garage. "Keys are over there. It's a perfect day to have the top down. Have fun. We'll do the dishes as payment for breakfast. It was great, by the way. I could get used to having you around."

Perry resisted saying "don't count on it." Instead she brushed her teeth, grabbed her wallet, and headed out the door before Campbell could change her mind and take back the offer to let her borrow her little Audi coupe. Campbell had always liked small, fast cars, but since high school Perry had faced a constant battle whenever she wanted to drive Campbell's car. Perry remembered standing in the garage yelling that she was never going to learn how to drive because Campbell wouldn't teach her, but the truth was she just hadn't wanted to learn in Justin's beater car, preferring to be seen in the Mazda RX Campbell had purchased. Things sure had changed. Nowadays she couldn't imagine spending that kind of money on a car. Driving around Austin in Campbell's car came with a sense of guilt, but she was willing to endure it for the chance to get around on her own for a bit.

Grace unlocked the lobby door and flipped on the lights, once again relishing the quiet of the building. She'd spotted Campbell's car in the parking lot, but when she walked by her office it was empty, and she figured Wynne had driven to happy hour last night and they'd pick up Campbell's car later. She was relieved to have the office all to herself and was looking forward to a few uninterrupted hours of productive work. She often worked on Saturdays, not necessarily because she had to, but because, as much as she loved Campbell and Abby, she enjoyed the silence of an empty building, free from phones ringing, machines whirring, and interruptions of any kind. The peace rejuvenated her, comforted her, and she was super productive when she was by herself.

The bad part was the alone time thing spilled over into the rest of her life and she wasn't sure how to break out of her shell. Sure, she spent time with her friends and her family when they were in town like tonight, but when it came to new adventures, like dating, it was easier to come here to the familiar rather than venturing out for the unknown. Campbell and Abby were constantly reminding her they'd left their big law jobs precisely so they could have personal lives, but after almost a year in their own firm, Grace was beginning to think this firm *was* her personal life, for better or worse.

Her phone buzzed and she instinctively reached for it, thinking it was probably her parents letting her know they'd arrived in town, but the text on the screen was from Danika. *Fun running into you last night. Hope to see you again soon. D*

Grace stared at the text for a moment. Should she reply right away or wait a bit so she didn't look like she was too eager? The question signaled just how out of touch she was with the wide world of dating. Surely she was overthinking her response. She started to type, *Great to see you too*, but then backspaced the letters until she was left with *Great*. Great indeed. If she couldn't even manage a simple text reply, how would she get through an entire date where she'd be expected to talk about something other than corporate happenstance?

"Are you going to stare at your phone all day?"

Grace nearly jumped out of her skin at the voice and she turned to face Perry who was standing in the hallway wearing a Greenpeace T-shirt and jeans. She looked casual and delicious at the same time, and Grace was almost too distracted by her sudden appearance and her inappropriate reaction to wonder what Perry was doing at the office on a Saturday. Almost. "How did you get in?"

Perry raised an eyebrow at the question. "Probably the same way you did. A key." Perry jingled a keyring as evidence. "Campbell loaned me her car and the office key was on the ring. I figured I'd get a head start on some of the records. That's okay, right?"

"Sure. Of course. Why wouldn't it be?" Grace wasn't sure why she was flustered, but she was and she didn't like it. Not here, in her sanctuary, not in front of Perry. "I'm going to work in my office. Help yourself to the war room."

"Thanks." Perry walked past her down the hall, pausing for a brief moment when they were mere inches from each other, but then moving on as if she'd never meant to linger. Grace wondered if she was the only one of them that noticed the heat that flamed up whenever they were physically close, and decided her imagination was working overtime. It had been way too long. Before she could give her reaction a second thought, she typed a return text to Danika. *Definitely fun. Are you free for Sunday brunch?* She hit send before her usual practicality could quell her spontaneity and the whoosh of the text was liberating. To avoid dwelling on the action, she tucked the phone in her pocket and settled into her office, determined to get through her to-do list before it was time to head home and change for dinner.

An hour later, she stared at her phone in exasperation. Danika had been sending all the signals, but now that Grace had taken the bait, she'd gone radio silent. Grace considered various legitimate reasons for Danika not to respond: a) she'd dropped her phone in the toilet, b) she'd been kidnapped, or c) she was one of those women who flirted but lost interest when the object of their affection became available. She wanted it to be a or b, well, mostly a, but she had a feeling it was c. Oh well, better she find out right up front that Danika was a fake than wasting any time putting on makeup and figuring out what to wear for a date to nowhere.

She stood up, stretched, and yawned. Coffee. She needed coffee. She took the long way through the office to the break room and stopped at the open door to the room where Perry was bent over a computer, staring at the screen. "Coffee break?"

Perry looked up and a slow, lazy smile slid across her face. "Coffee sounds great."

"Come on. I'm buying." Grace led the way to the break room and started working the levers to the espresso machine. "What can I get you? I think there's some soy milk in the fridge if you want a cappuccino or a latte."

Perry walked over and ran a hand along the side of the machine. "Wow. Fancy. Let me guess—Campbell bought it."

Grace laughed. "Yes, she did. Your sister has a penchant for fancy things."

"She always has."

Grace heard Perry's voice drop and reached for her hand. "She's always been a generous person, even before the settlement. Campbell likes to spoil the people she loves. When we opened this office she wanted to make it look like we were already very successful with things like this espresso machine and the hand-crafted marble table in the conference room. Mostly the trappings were to attract new clients, but partly to make Abby and me feel like we hadn't just walked away from high-paying jobs to start completely over with nothing. I'm pretty sure Campbell would rather have your parents back than all the money in the world."

Perry nodded. "I know you're right. And I get that having too much money is a silly thing to complain about. It's just that sometimes when I see all the things, it brings up why we have the money in the first place."

"What will you..." Grace stopped before she could finish, but Perry motioned for her to continue. "What will you do when you come into your trust?"

"I hate to admit I've already thought about it, but I've kicked around a couple of ideas. One is to fund my own team with Lawyers for Change."

"How would that work?"

"I'd still have to go through headquarters for project approval, but I'd have a lot more say in how we'd do the work and how long we'd stay at any one job. My money will only go so far, but I've been researching how to set up a foundation. I'd use the trust as seed money to convince others to donate. Plus, I could apply for grants to fund specific projects."

Grace was impressed. "Sounds like you really know a lot about what's involved."

"I'm sure there's a lot more to know, but I have a good handle on it. One of my professors does a lot of work with nonprofit foundations, and she offered to help me out when the time comes.

To be honest, I started talking to her about it because I had a crush on her, but she's the real deal."

The mention of a crush gave Grace a slight twinge of discomfort, but she couldn't pinpoint why so she brushed past it. "Your parents would be proud."

"Tell that to Campbell. She thinks I'm wasting my life, not to mention my education. But," Perry pointed at the espresso maker, "In some of the places I've been, a family of four could live for six months off the price of that machine. I know I keep repeating these analogies, but it keeps things in perspective for me."

Grace started to tell Perry she had a similar machine at her house, but decided defensiveness was not the tack to take. "I hear you, but everyone fills the void in their own way." She watched Perry take a deep breath and nod.

"Makes sense. I never really thought about Campbell having her own weirdness about the money and gifting it to absolve some of the guilt. She's always seemed so put together, it's hard to imagine her feeling insecure about anything."

"You two should talk sometime."

Perry laughed. "Now you're going too far." Her expression sobered. "We do talk, just not about anything important, unless she's trying to get me to be her version of responsible. It's been weird for me having a sister and a brother that feel more like parents. Really fucks with the dynamic."

"I'm sure," Grace said, but truthfully, she wasn't sure at all how Campbell, Justin, and Perry had managed to work out the balance of family without their parents. Campbell had been devastated when her parents died, but she didn't show it to anyone besides Grace and her brother, insisting she had to hold it together for Perry's sake. The funny thing was Perry did seem to have it together. Yes, she'd lost her passport, but that was because she'd had to make a quick getaway in the middle of the night, not due to being an irresponsible tourist unable to keep up with her belongings. Perry's work with Lawyers for Change wasn't conventional law practice, sure, but it was definitely more substantive than the work most law school graduates were doing within several years of getting their JD, and definitely meatier than the work Grace was having her do now.

They walked back to the war room and Grace pointed at the computer. "Find anything interesting?"

"Do you really want to know?"

"What's that supposed to mean?"

Perry handed her a legal pad. "I made a list of questions I would ask Hadley, you know, if I were in charge of this litigation."

Grace skimmed the list. *When did you realize the internal regulations and policies you have in place regarding the disposal of waste were deficient? Why don't you have internal controls to ensure you are complying with state and federal guidelines regarding the disposal of construction materials?* The others were in a similar vein. Perry's questions were pointed and provocatively worded, but clearly designed to prepare her client for a heated interrogation from the other side. "Do you already know the answers to these?"

"Most of them." Perry gestured toward the boxes of documents. "And if opposing counsel has read the discovery, then they do too. The question is whether your client knows what was really going on at his company."

Grace scanned the list again and made a snap decision. "Let's find out together. I'll schedule a meeting for next week. Does that work for you?"

"You want me there?"

"It's your list. I want to talk a little about tone first. We don't have to be the adversary to prepare him to deal with one. The goal is to get the client to confide in us, and to do that, we have to get them to trust us first. Bringing out the hammer is for the other side. Make sense?"

"I guess so."

"I'll show you when we meet with Hadley. But in the meantime, I think we should call it a day."

"You have a date or something?"

Grace rolled her eyes. Danika still hadn't texted back. She'd convinced herself she didn't care and right now she didn't. She was, however, enjoying Perry's company and wasn't eager for their newfound closeness to end so abruptly. "I do have a date. With my parents. Want to come with? I could really use a buffer."

"Buffer, huh? Your parents are great."

"That's what everyone says who doesn't have to live under the constant scrutiny of political life." Grace warmed up to her own idea and was convinced having Perry along would be the perfect way to have a smooth dinner with her parents, especially since Perry's ideals were more closely aligned with her father's. "Seriously, we're going to a nice dinner and they're paying. You'd be doing me a big favor."

"Well, when you put it like that, how can I possibly resist?"

"Great. Let's bug out of here. I'm headed home to change and I'll pick you up at Campbell's at six. It's not super fancy, but—"

"But you want to make sure I'm wearing something other than jeans and a T-shirt. Got it."

"Thanks."

A few minutes later as they walked out of the building together, Grace felt lighter and happier than she had all day.

Chapter Eleven

Perry came downstairs to find Campbell and Wynne in the kitchen fixing dinner. Once again, she noticed the way they maneuvered around each other, sharing the space with ease.

"Where are you going looking all spiffy?" Campbell asked.

"Dear Campbell, words like spiffy make you sound geriatric."

Campbell laughed. "Sometimes I feel that way. I heard everything the wedding planner said today, but I'm still trying to process how much we have to do before the big day. Thank goodness Roxanne is helping us out."

"I want to hear all about it, but I have dinner plans. How about I make brunch in the morning and you two lovebirds can tell me all about it?"

"Dinner plans? Moving pretty fast, aren't you?"

"It's Grace." Perry laughed nervously when she caught the odd expression on Campbell's face. "We're meeting her parents." Realizing she was digging a hole, she filled in more unnecessary detail. "I think it's a ruse for her to get me to work off the clock. I ran into her at the office earlier today, and we were talking about the case and she invited me to join them tonight. Didn't I mention I was going to work today?" Perry stopped talking, conscious of her own rambling. "What? You think it's weird, don't you?"

Before Campbell could answer, the doorbell rang and they all looked in the direction of the door. Wynne stood. "I think I'll get this while you two sort out...whatever."

Wynne had barely cleared the room, before Perry felt Campbell's hand on her arm, pulling her farther back into the house. She shoved Campbell away. "Seriously, what's your problem?"

"You don't think it's a little strange that you're headed out to dinner with the woman who is basically your boss?"

Campbell's authoritarian tone rubbed Perry the wrong way. "I wasn't aware that you had to approve Grace's social calendar. And she's not really my boss. I mean, I guess she is technically, but we both know this job is you trying to keep me busy while I'm stuck here. Maybe you can tell me what to do at work, but we're not at the office."

"I don't know. It seems a little weird."

"I thought you were all one big happy family. Besides, it's Grace." Perry wanted to admit it felt weird to her too, but not in the way Campbell meant. She'd felt weird since the moment Grace had asked her on whatever this was, but in a tingly, excited kind of way. The kind that made her spend an extra half hour to get her hair to sweep up to the side just right and had her standing in front of her closet way too long in search of exactly the right outfit to wear from her sparse collection of clothes. She'd settled on light tan chinos, a navy linen blazer, and a sky-blue shirt with a cowgirl pattern—an old favorite that had been in the bag of clothes Justin had brought over. She was pretty confident she looked okay for most people, but what if Grace preferred a more traditional look? Maybe she should've gone shopping for a suit? Dammit. It wasn't like her to second-guess so much, and maybe Campbell was right, but for the wrong reasons.

Hell no. She'd spent her youth dreaming of an evening out with Grace—and a lot more. Maybe a pseudo business dinner with the parents was the closest she was going to get, but she wasn't going to pass up the opportunity because Campbell couldn't release the reins.

"Here's the deal," she said. "It's not weird. You sent Grace to England to bring me home and we bonded over the experience. Just because she's your friend, doesn't mean she can't be my friend too. I've known her as long as you have, and I've met her parents before. The only one who is making this weird is you, and I think it's because you're jealous."

"I'm not jealous. Why would I be jealous?" Campbell said, looking genuinely surprised at the assessment.

"I dunno. We haven't spent much time together since I've been back," Perry said, feeling a twinge of guilt for effectively changing the subject, but plowing forward anyway. "You've been busy with your case and the wedding prep. I guess I should stick around and we can catch up."

Campbell glanced back toward the front door and then faced her with a contrite expression. "No, you should go. I don't know what I was thinking. Forgive your controlling sister and have a great time."

Perry started back toward the front of the house but stopped to hug Campbell. "I do appreciate everything you've done for me. You know that, right?"

"Of course." Campbell squeezed her tightly and whispered. "Be careful or you'll start to like it here."

Perry laughed and eased out of Campbell's embrace. "You just like my breakfast concoctions," she said in an attempt to add levity to what could quickly turn into an awkward conversation about her future plans. "Let's schedule some cooking lessons. I'll teach you everything I know."

Campbell's expression dimmed for a quick second, but she said, "Yeah, sure. I'm up for that." She jerked her chin toward the front of the house. "Shouldn't you be getting out of here?"

Perry led the way, the confidence in her step belying the bundle of nerves bunching up her insides. Okay, so this wasn't a date, but she'd fantasized so many times about what a date with Grace would be like, she couldn't help but go there. In her fantasy, though, she'd be the one pulling up to Grace's house, taking her hand, walking her to the car, and holding open the door. And then, after a fantastic dinner, which they'd abandon half eaten, they'd go back to Grace's place, and…Her dream date skidded to a stop at the very real image of Grace standing in the foyer wearing a scarlet dress, more flowy and definitely shorter than anything she'd seen her wear before. Perry's thoughts tumbled out of control. She was about to go out with this smart, accomplished, gorgeous woman, and, fantasy or not, she was determined to make the most of their time together.

Once they were in the car, Grace drove down the street ostensibly avoiding meeting her eyes.

"Is something wrong?" Perry asked, praying there wasn't.

"Campbell seemed like she had something on her mind. Is there something up with her?"

"Uh, no. I don't think so," Perry said. "She and Wynne met with Roxanne and the wedding planner today. Maybe it's stress about all the planning."

"I guess. Weddings are a big production."

"Too big if you ask me." Perry caught her eye. "Please don't tell Campbell I said that."

"Not the marrying kind, are you?"

"No. I mean, I don't know. Maybe."

"Well, I see you've given it a lot of thought."

"I'm not necessarily opposed to marriage, although its roots are steeped in patriarchy. Especially all the wedding rituals. The father giving the bride away, the dowry, the honeymoon was originally designed to be a time for the husband to impregnate his new wife so they could start making babies as quickly as possible so she could fulfill her other role as breeder."

"Wow, you're full of flowers and romance, aren't you?"

Perry grimaced, realizing she'd come on pretty strong. "Sorry."

"Don't be. If you don't want to get married, no one's making you." Grace's voice had a definite edge. "I mean, it's not for everyone. No judgment here."

"I'm not saying I wouldn't ever get married, but it would look a lot different from the traditional marriage. Equal roles and support for each other's dreams, even if that meant we didn't live in the same place, do the same things."

"You *have* given this some thought."

"I'm not immune to the allure of romance." Perry laughed at Grace's dubious expression. "Okay, I realize that made me sound like I was on the set of *Pride and Prejudice*. Seriously, though, I'm not a total brute. I may not have found anyone I want to spend the rest of my life with, but I'm open to it as long as they're open to something untraditional."

"That sounds suspiciously like someone who wants to have someone at home and another on the side."

Perry laughed. "Who has time for that? I have a lot I want to do with my life, and none of it involves staying at home."

"Okay." Grace stared straight ahead, ostensibly watching the road, but Perry could feel a slight chill settle into the air between them. Definitely not the atmosphere she wanted to cultivate. Eager to warm things back up, she shifted the focus back to Grace. "What about you?" she asked.

"Are you asking if I want a white picket fence and two children?"

"Sure."

"Not in the way you mean, but I do want security and stability and someone to share it with."

"Now who's the romantic one?"

"I'm plenty romantic, but I'm practical first. No sense getting all mushy about someone who isn't right for you."

Perry wanted to jab at Grace's functional view of love, tease her about talking about romance like it was a business venture, but she didn't really have any room to talk since her approach wasn't that much different. They both wanted very specific things when it came to the subject of love, romance be damned. She wanted a relationship that flouted tradition and Grace wanted contractually assured happiness. Their interests could not be more divergent, and the revelation took a bit of the thrill out of this date. Maybe it wasn't a date after all.

❖

Grace handed the keys to the valet and stepped out of the car, craning her head to see if she could spot her parents. She probably should've let them know she was bringing Perry along. She doubted they'd care—her dad loved to talk to anyone who'd listen, but if they did have something personal they wanted to discuss, then the addition of a guest would be a signal to hold off until after dinner. Hopefully, this dinner was simply a chance to catch up.

Her ruminating begged the question of why she'd invited Perry in the first place. She knew she wasn't the only one surprised at the move. Campbell had acted off about it when she'd showed up on her doorstep, and she could hardly blame her. In all the time she'd known them both, she'd never spent any alone time with Perry.

She wanted to believe the spontaneous invitation was a way to keep dinner light, but she knew it was more than that. She'd formed a bond with Perry while they were in London, and it had carried over when they returned home. Perry was fun and smart and cute. She watched her climb down from the SUV and reassessed. Perry wasn't cute. She was striking and full of youthful confidence. Who wouldn't be attracted to all that?

Shoving away her thoughts to examine later, Grace circled the car and joined Perry at the door to the restaurant.

"Any tips for tonight?" Perry asked.

"Yes. When in doubt, agree with my father. It's easier than listening to a filibuster on whatever."

"We got this." Perry hooked her by the arm. Grace's first thought was she should pull away, but it was quickly replaced by the comfort of the embrace. What was going on here? Was Perry simply being friendly or was there some shifting undercurrent between them? Was Perry feeling it too or was she oblivious to whatever was brewing beneath the surface of their friendship?

Grace didn't want to pull away, but she knew she should, and definitely before they encountered her parents who were nosy and would definitely get the wrong idea. "I'll check to see if they're here yet." She patted Perry on the arm and slipped out of her embrace, instantly missing the warmth of her closeness while relieved she didn't have time to analyze her reaction to it.

The concierge stand was crowded, and when Grace finally managed to cut through the crowd, the harried man working there didn't bother with courtesies.

"Reservation?" he asked briskly.

"Yes, Maldonado, party of four." She watched the man type furiously on his tablet and then glance back up at her with a frown. "I called to confirm earlier today," she said.

"You added another person to your party."

"Yes. Is that a problem?"

"It might be."

Perry appeared at her side. "What's wrong?"

"Nothing, just a little mix-up," Grace said. "What do we need to do to fix this?"

"You'll have to wait. You can go to the bar and I'll let you know when we're ready for you." The man looked back down at his tablet, clearly dismissing them.

Grace waved a hand in front of his face. "I'd rather sort this out now. My original reservation was for three people, correct?"

"Yes."

"And if I showed up with a party of three, you'd have a table ready for me, right?"

He scanned his tablet. "I would. You see—"

Grace raised her hand to stop him. "I'm looking around here, and I don't see any tables that only seat three people. I do see plenty of tables that seat four that aren't full. I'm thinking your manager would believe that having a four-top full is better than an almost full four-top. Agreed?"

He followed her gaze into the main dining room and slowly nodded his head. "Fine. Is your entire party here?"

Grace turned toward the door, relieved to see her mom and dad walking toward them. "Yes, we're all here."

Again, the man followed her gaze and he came to attention at the sight of Senator Maldonado approaching. She was used to the attention her dad always garnered when he entered a room. His commanding presence was one of the reasons he'd been elected and reelected to public office over the years, and she respected it despite the distance it placed between them. Senator Maldonado usurped the role of father more times than she cared to count, but she'd managed to reconcile the two roles into a manageable mix.

Her mother hugged her. Grace motioned to Perry. "Mom, you remember Perry, Campbell's sister."

"Yes, but the Perry I remember was a little girl. Look how grown up you are." Grace caught Perry bristle slightly at the word "little," but as her mother ran a hand along the lapel of Perry's jacket in a show of affection, her shoulders relaxed and she smiled. "It's great to see you, Mrs. M."

"Always so polite, this one. How is Campbell?"

"She's doing very well and sends her regards."

Grace watched their exchange, surprised at how quickly Perry went from rebel to suck-up in the presence of her parents. "Do you think Dad is going to join us anytime soon?"

The three of them turned back to see him still shaking hands with the other waiting patrons. He looked up and caught her watching him and strode over. "It's good to see you, my favorite daughter," he said, using the tired, but reliable joke since she was the only girl child in the family. He pulled her into an Insta-worthy embrace. "Are they ready for us?"

The host appeared at that moment, all smiles now that he knew they were someone important instead of mere peasants vying for a table with the rest of the masses. He showed them to a secluded booth far from the teeming crowd at the front of the room. Grace followed along behind, trying not to grouse about how a made in advance reservation wasn't good enough to be honored by the restaurant on its own.

"Are you okay?" Perry whispered, placing a hand on her elbow.

"Sure. Yes. Of course."

"You should practice not frowning when you say that. It would make your words a whole lot more convincing."

Grace rolled her neck and attempted a smile. "Sorry. Dinner with Dad makes me tense."

"I can see that. No worries. I'm here to be your support. We got this."

Perry sounded calm and self-assured and her confidence infused Grace with some of her own along with a heavy dose of gratitude. "Thanks. I really do appreciate having a buffer."

"Happy to be whatever you need."

Perry's tone was laced with innuendo, and Grace was certain it wasn't just her imagination. If Perry was anyone else, she'd be tempted to reciprocate, but acknowledging Perry's flirtation in any way would only encourage her and she had no business doing that. No matter how cute Perry looked tonight.

Once seated, they ordered drinks and Grace attempted to steer the conversation to safe ground. "I saw that the immigration bill you sponsored with Senator Murphy sailed through. Congratulations."

Her dad reached into his suit pocket and fished out a pen. "There were so many people involved with the bill, the president used a different pen to sign each letter of his name. "I had to fight Murphy for the M, but I won." He rolled it between his fingers, and then handed it to her. "I know it's only a pen, but this victory symbolizes a way forward for many people who haven't had a voice." He patted his heart. "I'm keeping it right here to remind me how privileged I am—we are—that we didn't have to fight for the freedoms we enjoy."

Grace murmured her agreement, certain he'd repeated the story many times to many people before this telling. She'd heard the sentiments a thousand times before, and after a while, the words lost their shine with replication. It wasn't that she didn't champion immigration issues or other social justice causes, but she did so quietly, choosing to speak with cash donations rather than taking center stage. Whenever she was persuaded to attend one of the many benefits throughout the year, inevitably she was cornered by well-meaning folks begging her to serve on their board. She knew she was qualified, but she also knew they weren't asking her because of any talents she might possess. Rather, they wanted the cachet that came from having a powerful senator's daughter to prop up at fundraisers as evidence of their reach.

The waiter reappeared to take their order, and Grace ordered the most expensive steak on the menu, partly because she'd read it had garnered excellent reviews in *Bon Appétit*, but partly to get under her father's skin since she knew he never ordered anything more expensive than the mid-range of the menu in order to keep his everyman image.

"Interesting choice," he said. "Perry, what would you like?"

Perry ordered a pasta dish after asking the waiter a couple of questions to make sure it contained no meat.

"And we'll split the salmon," Grace's dad said, indicating her mother. He handed the menus to the waiter and focused his attention on Perry. "Perry, is being a vegetarian a social choice or a dietary one?"

Grace braced for what was sure to be a lecture.

"Is there a difference?" Perry asked. "I mean all diets are related to social conscience. For example, what we choose to eat is often a function of not only geographic and economic circumstances, but also cultural ones, whether moral or merely embracing tradition. Sunday roasts, Friday fish, Monday beans." She paused and gave them a lopsided grin. "Sorry, I have a tendency to go on. But to answer your question, I feel better physically and mentally when I don't eat animal products. I'm not perfect about it—but I do my best. Believe it or not, it's easier when I'm traveling since most of the places I've been meat is not the central protein at each meal. It's definitively a privilege Americans enjoy more than the rest of the world."

Grace shifted in her seat, wanting to poke holes in Perry's argument, but she'd made good points and had obviously impressed her father—not an easy task. Instead she decided to change the subject. "Are you staying in Austin for a while?" She directed the question to her mother.

"A few days at least, and then we have a slate of events planned. It's a large constituency and your father has town halls scheduled around the state before the next session convenes."

She'd expected as much. The citizens of Texas were the firstborn children in the Maldonado family, sucking all of the attention out of the room, leaving little time and energy for her. She was being a bit of a baby, but she couldn't help but wonder what her life would've been like if her parents had had normal careers, the kind where they came home at the end of a day at the office instead of spending evenings and weekends raising money and networking for the next big thing. "Thanks, then, for making me the first stop on your tour," she said, striving to keep any tone out of her voice.

"It was definitely planned," her dad said. "We have some news. Perry, can you keep a secret?"

Perry grinned. "Isn't that the main skill lawyers are required to possess? You bet."

Her dad raised his glass in one hand and grasped her mom's hand with the other. "Next week, we plan to announce my candidacy for governor of Texas."

Grace had started to raise her own glass for the toast but stopped midair as the words slammed against her brain. "Governor?"

"Yes. Isn't it exciting news?"

He tilted his glass toward hers, but her hand was frozen in place while her brain whirred out of control. "I'm not sure exciting is the word I'd use. Surprising, bewildering might be more accurate. What about your work in the Senate?"

"Big picture, Grace. As governor, I'll be in a better position to do good things for the people right here at home without the scrabbling and infighting of DC politics. Besides, I could do with a little executive experience on my résumé."

Executive experience. Grace rolled those words over in her mind a few times, but she was certain she understood the code. "You're preparing to run for president."

He looked almost impressed that she'd figured out his master plan, but his words were classic politician. "I'm preparing to do a fantastic job as the next governor of Texas. We'll do great things here."

Grace turned to her mother. "What do you think about this?"

She placed a hand on Grace's arm in a move that was probably supposed to be comforting. "Your father does important work. I'll be right there with him every step of the way."

"You both realize that if Dad becomes the governor, I'll be conflicted out of a major chunk of my regulatory business?"

"Think of the big picture, Grace. We all make sacrifices for the common good."

Grace wanted to scream, but she knew it would accomplish nothing. Her parents had never left her wanting for food, clothes, or shelter, but when it came to more esoteric needs, they would always put the needs of the "citizens" ahead of hers. She caught Perry's eye and saw sympathy and compassion—huge for someone who might point out that she was lucky to have parents at all, let alone such accomplished ones. And she should be grateful for them, but right now the only thing she was grateful for was having Perry at her side when her father dropped his bomb.

CHAPTER TWELVE

L et's go to Birdie's and grab a drink," Perry said as they left the restaurant. "That was super intense, and I think we both could use one."

"What I should do is go home and burrow," Grace said. "It's late for an old-timer like me."

"As if." Perry wavered for a moment. She wanted to push, but she didn't want to push Grace away. It was a delicate balance and she wasn't used to being delicate. She chose her words carefully, not bothering to examine why she felt the need to tread carefully with Grace when if it were anyone else, she would railroad them until she got what she wanted. "You'll feel better if you process some of that before you go to sleep. I promise."

Grace reached for her hand and squeezed. "When did you get to be the wise one?"

"I've always been this way. When did you start to notice?"

In the shadow of the light outside the restaurant, Grace's expression morphed from lines of stress to a warm glow of radiance. Perry was completely captivated, unwilling and unable to look away and unaware of anything else around them. Beats of silence passed, but their eyes remained locked, holding them in an uncertain embrace.

"Do you have your ticket?"

Perry silently cursed the valet who'd wandered into the middle of their moment. She watched as Grace produced the ticket and a generous tip, and when the SUV came round, she brushed off the second valet who tried to open her door, eager to get back into the bubble with Grace.

"Maybe one drink would be a good way to unwind," Grace said as she pulled out of the parking lot.

"Trust me on this." Perry held back a self-satisfied smile, unwilling to count her victories until she had Grace in the club, ready to relax. "You look fantastic and it'd be a waste not to show off that dress." A moment of awkward silence hung in the air after her words and, anxious to fill the space, she rushed to say, "Besides, it's still early enough that it shouldn't be too loud. You know, for your sensitive older woman ears."

Grace play slapped her. "You're hilarious."

"It's one of my many desirable traits."

"You're supposed to let other people say things like that."

"I learned to be self-sufficient at a young age." Perry laughed to cover the spike of pain at the reference to her parents' death.

"Don't do that."

"What?"

"Go for the punchline at the expense of your feelings." Grace turned into the parking lot for Birdie's. "You suffered a big loss, in some ways more so than Campbell and Justin because your parents weren't around when you probably needed them the most. And I'm just now realizing how rude it was for me to ask you to come to family dinner tonight. How insensitive am I?"

Perry's heart melted at the sympathy reflected in Grace's eyes. "You're not insensitive at all. Other people's parents are more of a comfort than a painful reminder. If anything, tonight reminded me not to romanticize everything I didn't have. For all I know, Mom and Dad would've lost their minds at the thought of me traipsing around the globe, living in third world countries after they worked hard to pay for law school. I was lucky to have the time with them that I did, and while their deaths made no sense in the scheme of the universe, I have to believe it wasn't entirely senseless even if I can't figure out the reasons and even if I'm a little screwed up because of it."

"Perry Clark, you're pretty damn smart."

"I know, right? And my smart meter is telling me we should go inside before that security guard over there shines his flashlight through the window." Perry scrambled out of the SUV before Grace could make another remark about how she used levity to cope. The grief she felt about her parents' death was always right below the surface, especially when she was back in Austin, but there was something different about this time and she was certain that something was Grace. She couldn't quite wrap her mind around why though. Grace had been in her life for a very long time, and her memories of her were deeply rooted in family, but being around her now was different, refreshing, new. Was it her imagination their relationship had shifted or did Grace feel it too?

"Ready?"

Grace was standing close, and just like outside the restaurant, Perry was transfixed by her beauty and the warmth of her smile. *Don't ruin this moment by overthinking it.* She looked down at Grace's outstretched hand and shoved her second-guessing away. Friends held hands all the time. No big deal. She grasped Grace's hand in her own. "Absolutely."

The bar was as packed as it had been the night before, but everything about the atmosphere was different. The top forty pop mix had been replaced with club-style techno beat, and a machine pumped in a haze of white smoke. Other women checked them out as they walked through the crowd with equal glances of approval and jealousy at their clasped hands. Perry cast a sidelong glance at Grace who seemed not to notice the attention they were drawing, but she reveled in it like the nerd who'd been asked to the dance by the prom queen. She pointed out a table where the occupants were leaving. "Grab that and I'll get us some drinks."

Grace made her way to the table and Perry took a moment to watch her go, allowing herself to imagine what it would be like if this really were a date, and then she remembered she'd suggested this outing so Grace could decompress from dinner with her parents, not for her to exercise her dream date fantasies. She ordered a couple of Manhattans from a femme young bartender who didn't bother to card her.

"You're a lifesaver," Grace said, taking a deep drink from the glass. She fished the cherry out and popped it in her mouth. "I usually let these sit in the bottom of the glass and soak up all the bourbon, but tonight I don't feel like delaying my gratification."

From your lips. Perry murmured her approval and downed a healthy dose of her drink. "You want to talk about it?"

"What's there to say? I love my parents, but I will never be first to them or even second. Sometimes I wonder if they had children because it was the politically expedient thing to do. You know, you have to draw in those family people and how can you do that without having some of your own."

She followed her remark with a half-smile, and Perry shook her head. "Nope. No covering up the pain. It's okay to be mad at your folks. I mean if you can't be mad at your family, who can you be mad at?"

"That makes no sense."

"Sure it does. The people you're the closest to are the ones most likely to get on your nerves. It's true. I don't make the rules."

"Noted." Grace pointed toward the dance floor. "I don't want to talk about my parents anymore. Let's go dance."

Perry struggled to look like it was perfectly normal that she and Grace would take to the dance floor together. She raised her glass. "Bottoms up."

Grace raised her glass and clinked it against hers. "To a good time."

"Cheers to that." Perry downed the rest of her drink, enjoying the warm slide of whiskey as it burned its way into her stomach. "Ready?"

Grace set her glass down and reached into her pocket. "One sec." She pulled out her phone and held it up. "This might be my parents." She stared at the screen, grinned, and typed a quick reply.

"What?"

"Not the parents."

"I figured, judging by the expression on your face. Good news?"

Grace set the phone on the table, facedown. "Nothing important."

Perry inclined her head, certain Grace was hiding something from her. "Then why do you look so giddy?" She grabbed the phone and turned it over in time to catch an incoming text and, disregarding the fact she was completely violating Grace's privacy, she jabbed at the message app and let the entire conversation fill the screen.

I've been stuck at a firm retreat all day. No phones allowed. Too late to take you up on your invite?

Good excuse.

Totally true. I promise. I'll even treat for brunch if you're still up for it.

Perry stared at the phone wishing she'd never seen the conversation between Grace and Danika, but not wanting to let it go in case there was more. There wouldn't be more of course unless she handed the phone back to Grace so she could continue the conversation. She met Grace's eyes, but couldn't quite read the expression there. "She's not right for you."

"And you know that how?"

Perry didn't have a good answer for the question. Her teenage self might have said something silly and romantic like "because I'm the one for you," but she didn't believe in soulmates and lifelong loves and all that crap because good things didn't last, and whether that belief was a by-product of her parents' death or not, it was true. So why did adult her have a problem with Grace being with someone else? She handed the phone back to Grace, stood, and pointed toward the dance floor in a challenge of sorts. "Let's dance." She strode away willing Grace to follow her into the haze of smoke and hard-hitting beats she hoped would distract her from asking questions she couldn't possibly answer.

She edged through the crowd, found a spot near the DJ booth less crushing than the rest of the room, and surrendered to the primal beat. Movement equated to freedom. Freedom from feeling trapped in Austin. From the memories being back here brought to life. Freedom from conflicted feelings about Grace.

A tap on her shoulder. She went still, and a moment later Grace was standing in front of her moving in slow motion to the bass pounding from the nearby speakers. Her movements appeared cautious at first, like this whole dancing thing was brand new, and Perry slowed her rhythm to match her pace. They were completely in sync when the music changed from hard pounding techno to a gentle ballad. Out of the corner of her eye, Perry could see first date couples peeling off the dance floor, leaving lots of space for lovers and drunks to sway to the slower pace. She refocused her attention on Grace and found her staring hard with a smoldering look in her eyes. Emboldened by being the center of her focus, Perry stepped closer into the circle of Grace's arms. Time was suspended as they stood with almost no space between them.

Perry reached her arms around Grace's waist and pulled her even closer until mere inches separated their lips. Had Grace's lips been so full, so lush when she'd crushed on her years ago? Had her deep brown eyes held this same combination of mystery and allure? How in the world had she been able to resist kissing her? Why hadn't the courage of youth catapulted her into seizing the day, or the lips as was the case here? If she couldn't do it then, could she do it now?

She leaned in and lightly brushed her lips against Grace's, then drew back and locked eyes with her, looking for permission for more. The consent was quick and clear. Grace pulled her closer, slid a hand up the back of her neck, and pressed her close. When their lips met again, the connection was electric, swift, and sure. Perry laced her tongue with Grace's and groaned at the off the charts pleasure that pounded throughout her entire body. As the kiss deepened, her arousal soared, and she wondered why, why had she waited this long to make the first move?

The music stopped and the DJ's voice sounded over the speaker. Perry tried to ignore the interruption in favor of the bliss of Grace's kiss, but Grace shifted in her arms. "Don't stop," Perry murmured against her lips, reluctant to break their embrace, but Grace squirmed free and took a step back. Her eyes were hazy with a half aroused, half shocked expression. "It's okay," Perry said, reaching for her hand. "Come here."

Grace shook her head. "I can't. This," she waggled a finger, motioning between them. "No."

Perry stepped forward, raising her hands in the air when Grace backed up farther at her approach. She motioned to a table near the edge of the dance floor and followed Grace there. Once they were seated, she repeated, "It's okay," hoping her assurance would stick.

"It's not okay. We can't do this."

"Why not?" Perry asked. Outright rejection she could handle, but Grace's physical reaction had made it clear Grace was as aroused as she was. "Tell me you weren't turned on just now."

"I wasn't. I mean I was, but that's not the point."

"Then what is it? What's stopping you from being with me? You have to know I've been crushing on you hard since you first showed up at our house with Campbell all those years ago."

"Perry, stop it."

She should honor the request. Grace was making it pretty damn clear she wasn't interested, and but for the fact her body's reaction had given her away, Perry would be forced to believe her. But people don't kiss like that when they're not interested, not aroused, not wanting more. The only other conclusion was that Grace was overanalyzing the situation instead of giving in to her feelings. She reached a hand across the table and traced a heart on the back of Grace's hand. "Don't overthink it. Let yourself have some fun." She grinned. "I promise you'll have fun."

Grace's eyes closed for a moment and Perry waited for her to succumb, but when they opened again, Grace's expression was sharp and stern. "You may live your life that way, but I don't. I think about the consequences of my actions and how what I do affects other people, people I care about."

"What's that supposed to mean?"

"It means not everyone measures everything in terms of how exciting it's going to be. We have roles. Technically, I'm your boss. I'm your sister's best friend. This is complicated. This," she wagged her finger again. "Isn't ever going to happen. Never. And no amount of super hot kissing is going to make it so."

"Wow. Never?" Grace's words were harsh enough, but she backed them up with arms folded across her chest and another stern look. Whatever switch the kissing had turned on was now solidly turned off, and Perry knew Grace thought now that she'd stated her reasons, she was done with her.

But they were dumb reasons because Grace wasn't really her boss and who cared what Campbell thought? Well, screw that. She wasn't going to sit around here pretending like whatever had just happened between them was a figment of her imagination, and she certainly wasn't going to be lectured about being a responsible adult. She wished she'd never admitted her feelings to Grace. Perry pushed away from the table and pointed at her chest. "I'm going. Why don't you text your pal from the plane and you can have a nice dull evening together?"

"Wait, don't go away mad." Grace looked pained.

Perry grinned to cover her vulnerability. "Oh, I'm not mad. You're the one missing out here."

"But I drove."

Seriously, were transportation logistics all Grace cared about? Was she worried Campbell would be mad if she didn't safely escort the kid sister home? The realization was like a stab to the gut.

"Oh, I have no doubt I can find a ride." Perry made a show of looking around the room. "I'm sure there are plenty of people here who have a healthy appreciation for a super hot kisser." She stared at Grace for a moment, unsuccessfully willing the last few minutes away. Her concentration changed nothing, and she turned and strode away, struggling not to turn back to see if Grace's eyes were on her, telling herself she didn't care either way.

❖

Grace pulled into her garage and sat in the car, still paralyzed by the scene back at the bar. From the kiss to Perry's abrupt departure, she couldn't seem to process exactly what had happened, but she knew one thing—her relationship with Perry had radically changed and she didn't have a clue what to do about it.

Perry had kissed her. Not a quick, friendly kiss, but a long, lingering, lover-like kiss. And she'd kissed Perry back, matching her passion in equal measure. What had she been thinking? Perry was her employee, her best friend's sister, the little kid who'd tagged along with her and Campbell everywhere they'd gone, annoying them and infringing on their adventures. But Perry wasn't a little kid anymore, and while her headstrong ways might be annoying, she was also smart, funny, and good-looking. If she were older, if she weren't Campbell's sister, Grace would swipe right in a heartbeat. And now that she knew what a fantastic kisser Perry was…Damn, she was in trouble. She needed to find a way to go back and purge the last hour from her memory as quickly as possible or she'd start to obsess about Perry's kissable lips and ways to connect with them again.

Her phone buzzed and she seized it and stared at the screen, hoping for an overture from Perry, but disappointed to find only a new message from her mother. *Thanks for dinner. I know these meetups are always a challenge, but we do appreciate you and everything you've become. Give our best to Perry and wish Campbell well on her wedding. Love you.*

She stared at the text and started several replies, but she kept stumbling over Perry's name and finally closed out of the app, promising herself she'd respond later when her skin wasn't still on fire from the way Perry had held her close. She thumbed through the rest of her texts on the off chance she'd missed one. She hadn't, but she did slow down and hover over the text from Danika that had prompted Perry to ask her to dance. *Too late to take you up on your invite?*

Brunch, right. She'd never actually responded to Danika about brunch tomorrow. It was eleven. Late, but not too late. Would Danika still be up? If she did respond, what should she say? "Hey, when I invited you to brunch, I hadn't yet kissed the new associate at our firm who I've known since she was a little kid running around after me and her sister, who happens to be my best friend. Now that I've kissed her, it's going to be hard for anyone else to measure up, but I'd probably be better off with a more appropriate relationship so maybe we should meet after all."

She laughed at the absurdity of her mental rambling, but it didn't take long before her laughter morphed into an idea. A date with Danika might be exactly what she needed to distract from what had just happened with Perry. A sit-down meal with a woman closer to her own age who had a stable job right here in Austin. Yes.

She composed the text before she could change her mind. *I am absolutely still in for brunch. Meet you at Magnolia's at eleven. Looking forward to seeing you.*

She hit send, but before she could stow her phone and get out of the car, it buzzed with Danika's response. *Perfect place. Looking forward to seeing you too.* She smiled at the response and resisted the urge to keep the conversation going. Twelve hours was a short time to wait and there was all that stuff about absence making the heart grow fonder. She didn't necessarily believe in the sentiment, but it might explain Perry's actions. It had been years since she'd spent much time with Perry, but she'd always kind of wondered if Perry had a thing for her—the way she followed her around and did all those attention-grabbing moves younger kids do when they were trying to impress someone. She'd done a few of those things herself back when she'd had a crush on her fifth grade teacher, Mrs. Donnelly. She'd stayed after class every Tuesday when she knew Mrs. D worked late, and volunteered to clean up the classroom, decorate bulletin boards, or straighten books— whatever it took to capture the crumbs of her attention away from the rest of the class.

Grace shook away the thought as she walked into her house. Perry wasn't a little kid sucking up to her favorite teacher. She was a grown woman, a lawyer, and perfectly capable of respecting boundaries and outgrowing any childhood crush she might have had. Besides, even if Perry's feelings were real and she were interested in reciprocating, Perry would be gone the minute her passport arrived in the mail. She was nothing more than a stopover distraction, but someone like Danika might be a potential pick for a future Mrs. Maldonado. Plus Grace knew Campbell well enough to know she wouldn't be too keen on her sister dating her best friend.

None of this should matter because she wasn't interested in getting involved with Perry in the first place. But that kiss…That slow, searing, seductive kiss had wound around her senses and lingered still. If she wasn't interested in Perry, then why had she had such a visceral reaction to her touch and why did she tremble at the memory even now?

CHAPTER THIRTEEN

Perry pulled up in front of Justin's house—the house where she'd grown up—and sat in the car, contemplating whether she should go in. She'd slipped out of the house before Campbell and Wynne woke, not wanting Campbell to read in her face anything about what had happened the night before, but not wanting to be alone either.

She stepped out of the car and breathed in the early morning air. It was early enough on Sunday morning that the neighborhood was quiet, but she took a moment to close her eyes and bathe in the memory of running down the street, playing tag with her friends on hot summer nights until way after dusk.

Grace had lived two streets over, close enough that she and Campbell practically lived at each other's houses. Until their parents died, and Campbell settled into the role of pseudo mom, running the household with Justin despite being a kid herself. Grace had spent even more time at their house then, hanging out with Campbell, and Perry's infatuation had only deepened with proximity. This block, this yard, this house was streaked with memories of days spent trailing around behind Campbell and Grace, trying to get Campbell to treat her like an adult and trying to get Grace to notice her.

It had been a mistake to come here so soon after being rebuffed. She was halfway to the door and started to turn around when the door opened, and Justin stood staring at her.

"Hey, P, are you coming or going? I need to know because I'm about to start the pancakes and I need to know if you want that flax seed stuff instead of eggs in yours."

"There are pancakes? Well, why didn't you say so?" She quickened her step and followed him into the house, and just like that, she was a kid again and Justin was taking care of her. With a twinge of guilt, she thought his methods didn't feel smothering as it did sometimes when Campbell tried to stand in the parent role. He was more about making sure her basic needs were met while Campbell had been focused on making sure she got into the right school, got the best grades, and the right job.

She'd done okay, not Campbell level okay, but she'd scored well enough to gain entry to a top tier law school, even if it wasn't the alma mater Campbell would've preferred. Richards College was still in-state, but far enough away that Campbell hadn't been able to drop in whenever she wanted to check up on her.

"The flax seed's in that cabinet over there," Justin said as they entered the kitchen. "Do your magic and I'll heat the griddle."

Perry pulled the bag down from the cabinet along with a small bowl. She mixed the flax seed in some water, whipped it up with a fork, and set the timer on her watch to allow it to set. "I'm kind of scared to ask, but is this the same bag you had last time I was here?"

He grinned at her. "Believe it or not, no. Is there a problem with me keeping some on hand?"

"On the off chance your wayward sister drops by? I highly doubt that's the reason." She pulled open the cabinet again and spotted several other ingredients familiar to her, but what she figured were foreign to her brother. "If I didn't know better, I'd think you're a closet vegan. What's up, bro?"

He waved a spatula at her. "Nothing, bro. It's possible, I might occasionally have a guest who doesn't eat meat."

"Sure, but this is next level preparation." A thought struck her. "Wait. You're seeing someone, aren't you? Only true love would drive you to shop for things off the beaten path." She grabbed him around the waist and started tickling him. "Tell me everything. What's she like? Or what's he like? It's been so long since I've seen you, I don't even know which way you swing."

"I'm still batting for Team Hetero."

"Not that there's anything wrong with that," Perry mimicked the joke she and Campbell used to have whenever people asked if their brother was gay too.

"P.S., it's not my fault you haven't been around."

Perry heard the tone and forced back a defensive retort. There really wasn't any point arguing the fact she hadn't been around. "I'm here now."

"And it's pretty great having you." He slid a tall stack of pancakes off the griddle. "Grab the margarine and syrup, will you?"

She complied, loving the easy way he welcomed her in without asking a bunch of questions about why she'd shown up on his doorstep on a Sunday morning. She foraged in the fridge and came up with the margarine and syrup and a variety of berries which she took to the table. "Plates in the same place?"

"Do I look like someone who moves dishes around?"

"Maybe your lady caller fancies having the dishes in a different place."

"Is there some reason you're talking like you're a cast member of *Downton Abbey*?"

"Is there some reason you know what a cast member of *Downton Abbey* sounds like?" Perry set the table for two and Justin joined her with the large platter of pancakes. "Seriously, I need to know everything."

"I met her at South by Southwest this year. She works for a production company that's been doing a bunch of work in the area. Believe it or not, they want to use ACL as a venue."

Perry poured a liberal dose of syrup over her pancakes. "Are you still volunteering there?"

"Every spare moment I can get."

Perry nodded and dug into her food. Justin was a big music fan and had worked backstage at the popular Austin City Limits venue as a volunteer for years. She had fond memories of him sneaking her backstage. "I'm guessing she got the secret Justin tour." She pointed her fork at her plate. "These are perfect, by the way."

"You know it and thanks. I've been perfecting my vegan breakfast offerings."

"Women drive a person to do all kinds of crazy things, am I right?"

Justin raised a forkful of pancakes. "Truth."

They spent the next few moments chewing in companionable silence, and Perry enjoyed the easy familiarity of her brother's presence. He'd always been the calm, easy-going presence in sharp contrast to Campbell's hard-driving push toward success. Not that Justin wasn't successful—he was—but he was low-key about it whereas Campbell was the splashy, rah-rah rainmaker encouraging everyone around her to be as driven as she was.

"Are you staying long?"

Perry considered purposely misunderstanding his question to mean was she hanging around today, but she knew he meant long term and it was a big deal for him to ask. Two days ago, she'd been leaning on staying until the wedding despite her earlier reservations, but after Grace's rejection last night, things around the office were going to be way awkward, but it wasn't like she could just up and quit without explaining why to Campbell. If her passport were here, she knew she'd be on the next flight out, but she was stuck until it came. Of course, she could travel somewhere else within the States. She had friends from school in Dallas who'd probably put her up for a week or so. But she'd made a promise to Campbell and a commitment to Grace who had saved her ass in London. "I don't know," she said, giving the best answer she could under the circumstances. "It's complicated."

"Most things are," he said. "You'll figure it out."

"Thanks, J."

"For the pancakes? No big deal to throw on an extra stack."

"For the pancakes, yes, but mostly for not pushing."

"She loves you, you know. She'd do anything for you."

Perry knew he was referring to Campbell. "I love her too, but I'm not her and no amount of trying is ever going to make me into a corporate lackey who thrives on tradition."

"Tell me how you really feel." Justin grinned. "Seriously, though, she just worries about you and the only way she can measure if you're okay is by her standard. Besides, she has a lot going on right now with the wedding."

"I know you're right, but like I said, it's complicated." Perry started to bring up her feelings for Grace, but while she trusted Justin to keep her secrets, she wasn't ready to examine her emotions out in the open. "Tell you what, I promise I'll be here for the wedding, but I can't commit to sticking around in the meantime or after. It's really hard to be here. I don't know how you live in this house day after day."

"It wasn't always easy. Right after Mom and Dad died, I wanted to be anywhere but here. I'd walk through the hallway and see all of the pictures of us as a big happy family and the extra space Mom left to hang more pictures—you know, for when we all got older. Knowing they would never be older and that if we ever have kids, they will never know their grandparents used to make me want to drive my fist through the wall. Sometimes it still does."

Perry stared at him, trying to imagine her calm, cool, laid-back big brother hitting anything for any reason. "You never showed it."

"No. You can thank Campbell for that. Yes, her perky optimism can be annoying, but more so it saved me from going down a dark hole of depression, worrying I wouldn't be able to keep us together and safe. I was the legal adult, but she was the grown-up in every way that matters, confident we could make it through anything and make Mom and Dad proud whether they were here to see it in person or not. I don't know if I could have been in charge of this family without her."

Perry let his words digest. She'd always seen Campbell as her bossy big sister who bested her in all the traditional measures of success, and she might still be all that, but apparently, there were layers she either didn't know or had been unwilling to see, but she still wasn't sure what to do with that information. "Thanks for telling me all that."

"Sure." He stood. "You want more pancakes?"

"Not if I want to fit in my clothes again." She leaned back in her chair and patted her stomach. "Why do I always want a nap after pancakes? You'd think they have tryptophan in them or something."

Justin heaped another stack of pancakes on his plate. "Definitely sends me into a food coma, but I've got a ton of work to do in the yard later, so I'm considering this necessary carb loading."

"Mom's roses are looking good." Perry's throat started to close up at the memory of her mother crouched in the garden, tending to her rose bushes.

"Thanks. You're welcome to stick around and help in the yard."

"I appreciate the offer, but dirt has never been my thing."

"I see how it is. You got your pancakes and you're done."

"How well you know me."

"Seriously, P, you didn't come here on the off chance I was whipping up brunch. Something's on your mind."

He'd always been able to read her, but he rarely pushed. She must not be hiding her angst as well as she thought she was. She could definitely use a sounding board, but she didn't even know where to start. "It's complicated."

"You keep saying that, but I've found 'it's complicated' is code for either I don't want to talk about it or I don't feel like doing the work."

"Harsh."

"Just calling it like it is."

He was right even if she wasn't used to him being so blunt with her about her hang-ups. "It's not that I don't want to talk about it, but I don't know what good it would do. I'm tangled up in an impossible situation and I can't see a way out."

"Kind of vague there, sis. If you give me a little more information, maybe we can figure it out together."

She considered the offer. He knew Grace—hell, she'd been a regular fixture at their house. She could trust him not to tell Campbell anything she shared with him, but she hadn't been lying when she said she wasn't sure where to start. She settled on a slightly more detailed version without sharing everything. "Say you had a chance to kiss your childhood crush and it was everything you dreamed it would be. And they kissed you back. And for a few minutes you were certain you were in sync, but then they woke up or whatever, and next thing you know you're getting kicked to the door." Not entirely accurate, but close enough.

"Well, my childhood crush was Miss West, my kindergarten teacher who was around twenty years older than me. If I ran into her now, I imagine she's a hot older woman and we'd make a stunning couple." He sighed.

She punched him in the arm. "Focus, dude. You totally forgot the she kicks you to the curb part. How do you win her over?"

"Besides my obvious charm and good looks?" He narrowed his eyes and stared at her hard. "You only had one childhood crush that I know of."

Perry squirmed in her seat under his intense scrutiny. "This is a hypothetical."

"Is not."

"Is too."

"You kissed Grace Maldonado?"

"No." Perry shook her head. She should have known it would take very few clues for him to guess the subject of her dumbass hypothetical. She met his stare with a defiance that lasted all of a few seconds until she crumbled like an unprepared lawyer in front of a no-nonsense judge. "Okay, yes. But we kissed each other.

It was mutual. Very mutual. Like she was totally feeling it, and then—"

"Stop. Back up. How did this happen? When and where?"

"That's not important. It's the after part that matters."

"Bullshit. I need context. I fed you pancakes, now you feed me information. Start talking."

She did. She told him every detail of the night before from the moment Grace picked her up for dinner to the uncomfortable time with Grace's parents to the kiss at the bar.

"You kissed her and then you stormed out?"

"We kissed. Both of us." She persisted in the explanation even though she realized she was starting to sound like a nutcase. "She told me it was a mistake, that it couldn't happen again. What was I supposed to do?"

"Stick around and work it out? Use some of those fancy lawyer skills you have and convince her to see things your way? Something, anything besides running away."

His words landed hard, and the implication was clear. She ran away from everything. Her parents' death, the memories in the streets of her hometown, her sister's shadow. "I guess there really wasn't any point. As soon as my passport gets here, I'll be gone."

She avoided his eyes but not before detecting the disappointment reflected back at her. She didn't know if he was disappointed because he'd miss her or if he regretted she'd turned out to be a sad human incapable of forming normal human relationships. Either way, leaving would be the best, least disruptive thing she could do for everyone involved.

Grace watched Danika talk to the waitress about the exact ingredients of the featured menu items and took the time to assess her. It would help if her eyes weren't slits from lack of sleep, but so far everything she saw confirmed her first impression. Danika was a force. A tall, blond, gorgeous force of a woman who didn't let anything get in her way, including gluten because she was having a long conversation with the waitress about it that involved eliminating most of the things on the menu from her brunch feast while Grace thought hard trying to remember a gluten she hadn't been able to embrace. The thought then spiraled into an epic trailer of what life would be like with a woman who eschewed all the gluten goodness in the world. No impromptu morning runs to fetch a dozen donuts from Kate's. Kate offered a few gluten free options, but Grace had eaten one by accident once and it tasted like cardboard beneath the tasty frosting. Italian food without garlic bread, sandwiches without her favorite whole wheat nutty loaf, and no more of those piping hot yeast rolls from the diner down the street from the office. Okay, sure, she never actually went on impromptu morning donut runs—that was more Campbell's thing, but the idea of having the opportunity curtailed left her feeling sad and empty—an emptiness only gluten could fill.

"Do you know what you want?" Danika asked in her sexy purr of a voice.

Grace pushed away her chaotic, gluten-free nightmare, and focused on the menu, trying to ignore the way Danika's question caused her mind to stray to how absolutely delicious Perry had looked last night at the bar. "I'll have the blueberry pancakes," she said, deliberately choosing the most gluten-y item on the menu and feeling a tad bit like a jerk about it.

Danika ordered breakfast tacos with corn tortillas, and the waitress left to turn in their orders. Danika settled back against the booth and sighed.

"Long week?" Grace asked.

"The longest. This brunch is by far the best thing that's happened to me all week. How about you?"

Grace started to agree, but it hadn't really been a long week. The time working with Perry had flown by, and aside from the fact she was no longer exploring the streets of London, it had been a good week overall. Well, except for her dad's bombshell announcement he was running for governor and Perry's abrupt departure last night after delivering a bombshell of her own, but Grace wasn't about to share either of these life-altering events with a total stranger, even one she was trying on for potential girlfriend status. She settled on vague, but cheery, first-date kind of sharing. "I've had a fairly easy reentry. Except for some jet lag, it's been very productive."

"Do you travel internationally a lot for your job?"

"No, not at all," Grace answered before she recalled she'd told Danika on the plane she was traveling for both business and pleasure. Explaining the real reason for her trip would involve talking about Perry, so she danced around the subject. "The trip to London was a one-off. A meeting with a lawyer I know about a matter I'm handling, but otherwise, most of my work is right here in Texas."

"I have a confession to make."

Grace braced for whatever Danika was about to say. "Really?"

"Yes. I confess, I googled you. Top of your class at UT Law. Left an impressive career with a prominent firm in Houston to form your own firm with your two best friends. The profile in the *Austin Business Journal* made it clear the three of you are the ones to watch in the Austin legal community. If I needed a lawyer, you'd be my first call."

Grace took a drink of water to avoid the embarrassment of the moment. It wasn't like she didn't google people, but Danika's detailed recitation of her findings was a bit much. Wasn't it? Or was she simply going to find fault with pretty much anything Danika said coming so close on the heels of kissing Perry?

Dammit. She had to stop thinking about that kiss. Soft, sexy lips. A slow burn flaming into an intense bonfire. She could not remember ever being that aroused, that ready to let the rest of the world fall away and lose herself completely. Everything about the kiss had been perfect. In the moment. But the moment had ended when Perry confessed she'd always had a crush on her, and now, in the light of day, Grace had to admit, without any equivocation, she'd always known it was true.

Had she unwittingly encouraged Perry? Had the trip to London been a misread overture, taken by Perry to mean she was interested in her as more than the little sister of her very best friend? Except Perry wasn't the only one who'd been doing the kissing last night. Perry might have made the first move, but she'd willingly, enthusiastically even, embraced the moment and given in to the delicious way Perry's touch had made her feel. Until she'd come to her senses and pushed Perry away. It had been the right thing to do. The sensible thing. She could be proud of the decision she'd made to keep her distance even if she wished the confrontation had gone more smoothly.

And now here she was sitting in a booth, at a cozy brunch with a woman who was a catch by any standard, unable to think about anything but Perry's kiss. She was in trouble for sure.

CHAPTER FOURTEEN

Perry stared out the passenger window of Campbell's car, barely listening to her drone on about the interrogatories she'd served and the deposition she was defending today. How had her life become this monotonous? Home to work and back again, five days or more a week. And for what? To defend corporations who would rather shell out more money to avoid liability than to simply make people whole. Across the world, Numeroff was sitting in a cell, waiting for a sentence likely to rob him of the better part of his life, and she was supposed to care about grocery cart malfunctions and construction companies with no regard for the environment?

Today was the two-week mark in her wait for her passport and her pathway far away from here. She couldn't be more ready. Less than a week ago, in Grace's arms on the dance floor at Birdie's, she'd flirted with the notion of staying in Austin to see if the blistering kiss they'd shared led to something more, but the moment Grace dispelled her of any delusions they could ever be a thing, she'd made the decision to get out of here as soon as she could.

It was the right decision. Grace clearly didn't want her around. She'd spent the week communicating by emailed memos and neatly printed Post-its left on her computer in the war room, detailing tasks to be completed with not a hint of the friendly banter they'd shared. Perry hated to admit she'd held the notes, scanning them for some acknowledgement they'd at least been friends, but no. She'd been relegated to employee, no special benefits included. Well, fuck that. She'd bide her time, but as soon as her passport came, she was out of here.

"Are you okay?"

Perry shook off her thoughts, surprised to see Campbell pulling into the parking lot for the firm. "Yeah, sure. What's up?"

"You've just been out of it this week. Like your head's somewhere else. I know I haven't been around much, but everyone's noticed."

Perry perked up. "Everyone? Did someone say something?"

Campbell grimaced like she wished she hadn't mentioned it. "Nothing specific. Just wondering if you're okay. I get this isn't what you want to do with the rest of your life, but working here isn't the worst thing, right?"

Well, it wasn't before I kissed your best friend/my temporary boss and she blew me off like it meant nothing. Perry forced a smile. "No, it's all good. Guess I'm feeling a little melancholy is all."

Campbell squeezed her hand. "I get it. I really do. Look, I should be able to take a break this weekend. Let's spend Saturday on South Congress. Vintage clothes, Amy's ice cream, Guero's. It'll be fun. And both Wynne and I are going to be home on Saturday night. Let's have dinner together. I'd like you to spend more time with my future wife."

"Sure, yeah, sounds good." Maybe it would be good for her to do something other than work and pine after Grace. It wasn't like her to pine, and the unnatural act was taking its toll. She opened the door and stepped out of the car.

"Say hi to Roxanne for me."

"Okay," Perry said, unsure why Campbell suddenly brought up Abby's girlfriend, but not wanting to prolong the conversation now that she'd managed to avoid answering Campbell's questions. "Try not to fall asleep at your depo."

Graham waved to her as she walked through the lobby and she waved back. The odd office manager was a bright spot in the day because he could be counted on to be consistent. More than she could say for anything else in her life. She strode through the office, relieved not to run into anyone else before she made it to her office, but when she arrived at her desk, she found a bright pink Post-it with Grace's easily identifiable precise penmanship. *Hadley meeting, eleven thirty a.m. Conference room.*

Perry looked down at her outfit. She'd gone dark today to suit her mood, and she wore her black RBG T-Shirt, khaki cargo pants, and black Chucks. She figured all she'd be doing was sitting in this back office, rummaging through documents, so what did it matter what she wore? Grace could have given her the courtesy of a heads-up if she was going to be included in a client meeting. But then again, this was the client who was engaged in illegal dumping so did it really matter how she looked? At least she wasn't breaking the law. And it wasn't like whatever she wore, she'd impress Grace. That ship had sailed.

At ten o'clock, the phone on her desk rang and she nearly shot out of her chair. No one had called her in the two weeks she'd been here, and she figured it was a wrong number, but it kept ringing, so she lifted the extension and said, "Clark here."

"Perry, I have an announcement to make." Graham spoke with his distinctive cadence. "Your guests are waiting in the lobby."

"Don't know what to tell you, Graham, but I'm not expecting any guests."

"Ms. Daly and her guest then. Ms. Daly insists she has an appointment with you this morning."

Daly, Daly. The name sounded familiar and Perry spent a moment searching her mind for where she'd heard the name before. Birdie's. The first night she'd gone out with Campbell, Abby, and Grace, and she'd met Roxanne Daly, Abby's girlfriend. Back when everyone at the firm had seemed like a big happy family, before Grace had started ignoring her. Campbell's parting words from this morning came rushing back—tell Roxanne hello. Apparently,

Campbell had known Roxanne would be stopping by, but why was Roxanne asking for her?

Deciding it would be easier to sort things out in person, she told Graham she'd be right there, and took the long way to the lobby to avoid walking by Grace's office.

Roxanne and an attractive brunette were chatting when she arrived at the lobby. "Hi, Roxanne. I think there's some kind of mistake. Campbell's not here."

"No mistake. Campbell set up the appointment, but we're here to see you." She gestured at the other woman who flashed her a big smile. "This is Stella Rivera, the best tailor in Austin. She's here to measure you for your tux."

"Tux? Tuxedo? You're kidding, right?"

Roxanne shook her head. "Campbell wanted to surprise you. Said you weren't big on dresses, but since you'll be the maid of honor, figured you'd want some dressy duds to wear. We can customize your suit however you'd like. Stella has a magic touch."

Perry spent a moment digesting the information, taking long, slow breaths to quell the desire to run. Attending Campbell's wedding was one thing, but actually being part of the ceremony was way beyond what she'd envisioned. Shouldn't Campbell have asked her if she wanted to be maid of honor? And what about Grace? Oh, crap. If she and Grace were both in the wedding party, how was that going to work now that Grace was barely speaking to her? Perry didn't know much about weddings, but wasn't maid of honor a job reserved for a person's best friend? Was Grace going to be even more pissed if she took the top spot by the bride's side?

You could ask the Bride's Best Friend since she's standing right in front you. Perry looked at Roxanne's face, all cheery and happy and supportive of the bride, and remembered she'd promised Justin she would try to cut Campbell some slack. Campbell was busy after all and maybe she'd meant to ask and simply forgotten in the swirl of work and wedding prep occupying her life lately. It was pretty thoughtful of Campbell to send a tailor—a hot tailor, at that—to make sure she was comfortable in whatever she wound up wearing for the big day, but it was also likely super extravagant. She spent a moment wavering before ultimately deciding a new suit was exactly what she needed to take her mind off Grace and the icefest between them. "Cool," she said. "Let's use the conference room."

Once they were in the room, Stella sat across from her, a sketchpad in hand.

"My usual process consists of talking to you about your style, sketching out some rough ideas, and then taking your measurements. I can have your garments ready in a week and we'll do the first fitting then."

"That seems fast," Perry said.

"It is lightning speed," Stella said with a delightful laugh. "But Roxanne is a dear friend, not to mention an excellent source of referrals, and I understand your presence is a bit of a surprise, a pleasant one for sure."

Perry glanced at Roxanne who ducked her head. Had Campbell told everyone she was likely to flake on the wedding? And had Stella's last few words been flirtatious? Many things to ponder, but right now she needed to focus because Stella was sitting in front of her with her pencil poised and ready to sketch. Roxanne cleared her throat and said something about checking in on Abby and she disappeared from the room. When she was gone, Perry ran a hand down the front of her shirt to her pants in a flourish. "As you can see, I'm very fashion conscious."

Stella laughed. "My work isn't about fashion. It's about style, and I can already tell a lot about yours. Would you like me to share?"

"Absolutely."

"You like what you like, and you don't really care what others think about your choices."

"Yes, but that seems a bit obvious." Perry was beginning to feel like she'd been gifted a session with a hack medium whose predictions were only as good as the intel they could glean from seeing what was right in front of them.

"You know what looks good on you, and that's important. Size does matter."

Perry returned her grin. "Also true. Anything else?"

"Simple is best. You don't mind standing out, but not for your clothes." Stella's hand moved over the sketchpad with quick, bold strokes, and the room fell silent while Perry watched her sketch, transfixed by the process. A few minutes later, Stella handed her the paper.

"Tell me what you think. Be honest."

Perry stared at the image on the paper. She didn't know the right terms to describe the fashion on the paper, but she knew what the tuxedo depicted was both classic and modern at the same time, and she wanted to wear it right freaking now. She let her mind wander to the big day and imagined for a moment escorting Grace to the front of the church where they'd assume their positions next to Campbell. On the way down the aisle, people would stare, and she'd feel a little bit bad they were drawing attention away from the brides, but secretly giddy at what a striking couple she and Grace made.

"I'm thinking midnight blue. It'll complement the color of the other bridesmaids' dresses without being too matchy matchy. You like?"

Perry sighed and came back down to earth where Grace was avoiding her and highly unlikely to be up for being escorted anywhere if she was the one doing the escorting. Still, the sketch of the tux was gorgeous, and she'd be a fool to turn it down. "I like very much."

"Excellent. I'll get your measurements and let you get back to work." She reached into her oversized bag and pulled out a small foldable step stool and set it in front of her. "I promise this is sturdier than it looks. Step up on here and I'll start with your legs."

That's what she said. Perry held back a giggle as Stella ran a measuring tape up her inseam. Maybe a close encounter with the hot tailor was exactly what she needed to get past this silly obsession with Grace. She'd go to the wedding looking like a boss and Grace would be sorry then she'd missed her chance.

"Excuse me, I thought this room was empty."

Perry glanced over her shoulder to see Grace standing in the doorway to the conference room, her arms loaded with files, but Grace wasn't looking at her. She was staring at Stella who happened to be between her legs at this very moment.

"Perry? What are you doing?" Grace asked.

Perry wanted to make a smart remark, but for once in her life she couldn't come up with anything to say. She and Grace were locked in a gaze, and Grace's expression had gone from surprise to shock to hurt in the span of a few seconds, and that last one had her wondering. Why would Grace be hurt when she'd been the one doing the hurting?

"I'm getting a tux. For the wedding," Perry blurted out. "No big deal."

Stella chose that moment to pop out from between her legs and wave at Grace. "Don't mind me." She resumed her measurements, likely missing Grace's withering stare, but Perry saw it.

"What's wrong?"

"Wrong?" Grace shook her head. "Nothing's wrong. Well, except I have a meeting in here soon and I'd like to set up beforehand."

Right, the meeting with Hadley. "I know. I can set up for you if you let me know what files you want me to bring. I'll do it as soon as Stella is finished with me." She twitched as Stella stretched the measuring tape along her torso, nearly grazing her breast.

"Shouldn't be too much longer," Stella called out.

"Take your time," Grace said. "I can manage on my own." She turned and stomped out of the room.

"Not that it's any of my business," Stella said, "but she seems stressed."

Grace did seem stressed and again Perry was surprised by Grace's emotions. Part of her wanted to go to Grace and ask her if everything was okay, but the other part was still smarting from the sting of rejection. What she should do was find some distance. She wasn't going to be here much longer, and once she was gone, she'd forget her infatuation and move on with her life. In the meantime, she needed to embrace the fact Grace Maldonado was an enigma, and the sooner she got over her the better.

❖

Grace worked, or pretended to, for the next hour, until it was time to head back to the conference room. She ran into Perry in the hallway who, despite her morning visit from a custom tailor, was wearing a T-shirt and cargo pants and carried nothing in her hands except her phone.

"What?" Perry asked, looking down at herself. "Did I put my shirt on inside out?"

Grace winced against the mental image of Perry, pulling off her shirt. Had she undressed for Stella? She scrambled for something to say that didn't have anything to do with clothes on or off of Perry. "Don't you want to bring something to take notes?"

Perry pointed at the notebook and pen Grace carried. "Like that?" She fished in her pocket for her phone, pulled up the notes app and turned the screen toward Grace. "Welcome to this century. Trust me, I've taken notes before."

Grace flinched at the remark. It wasn't the first time in her life she'd been accused of micromanaging, but she was agitated about this meeting and she wanted it to go well. Plus, she couldn't get the image of Stella crouched between Perry's legs out of her head which only amped up her stress level. She wanted to pull Perry aside and attempt to clear the air, but Graham was headed their way with John Hadley in tow. "That's him. Take my lead."

"Sure thing. Besides, what do I have to offer?"

Grace heard the edge in Perry's tone, but she didn't have time to address it before John was standing in front of them. She grasped his hand. "It's good to see you." She motioned to Perry. "This is our new associate, Perry Clark. She's been reviewing the documents in your case and I've asked her to sit in on our meeting today."

"Clark like the name on the building?" John asked.

"Different Clark," Perry said, extending her hand. "Nice to meet you."

Grace led the way to the conference room, relieved that Perry appeared to be on her best behavior even if she did look like someone who'd wandered in off the street to hang out in the office. All she had to do was get through the next hour, and then she could decompress. Far from Perry and visions of her in a tuxedo.

Ten minutes later, she'd barely gotten through her summary of the agency's case against Hadley before the meeting went off the rails. "We still have to complete discovery responses, but we're drafting the answers based on the information we've located in the documents you sent us. I'll need you to review the draft responses and sign them, early next week."

"Sounds good. I can count on you to make this go away, right?" he said. "You know we didn't do anything wrong."

Grace smiled and pivoted. "I know your intentions were good. My job is to convince the regulators that you're dedicated to making things right and you deserve an opportunity to match your actions with your intentions."

"It would help if you were honest with us."

Grace froze at the sound of Perry's voice and subsequent scowl forming on John's face.

"What's that supposed to mean?" he asked.

"Nothing," Grace said at the same time Perry said, "It's impossible for us to represent you if you insist on pursuing a defense that's not tenable. You say you were collecting materials to be recycled, but where's the proof? Based on the memos I've seen, it appears that excuse was concocted after the regulators started nosing around, not before."

Grace spoke more forcefully this time. "Perry, that's enough." She turned to John. "Obviously, we have some work to do, but I'm confident we can get this done for you."

But John was focused on Perry. "Tell me what you mean."

Grace watched while Perry laid out the information she'd found. Information John himself may not have been aware of as the CEO. Yes, the company had started looking into the state's program for recycling asphalt shingles and other materials to be used for highway and other state sponsored construction, but they hadn't done their due diligence to make sure the way they accumulated and stored the materials was in compliance with state standards, and they hadn't filed a letter of intent with the state in advance, making their accumulation of stuff look like the illegal dumping it was. The ensuing memos trying to explain away the circumstance made everything they'd done look like a cover-up.

"Where are these memos?" John asked in a loud voice. "Who wrote them?"

"You haven't seen them?" Perry asked with a hint of incredulity.

"Of course I haven't, but rest assured when I find out who wrote them and who kept them from me, there will be consequences."

"I'm going to insist on interjecting here," Grace said, shooting Perry a look that she hoped warned her to quit pouring oil on the fire. "John, you cannot go back to your company this afternoon and start firing people. We need to take careful, considered action to make sure we're not sending the wrong message to the regulators. Let's take a moment to regroup."

"I don't know," Perry said. "Cleaning house might be exactly what needs to be done to show the regulators you're serious. If you really want to participate in the recycling program, do it the right way and start by terminating anyone who would thwart you. And if you're really serious about recycling, why not donate to a local effort to show you mean business? There are all kinds of good causes you can contribute to that would not only help your image but might actually make your customers feel like your company is a responsible community citizen."

Thwart you? Grace full on glared at Perry now, determined the next step would be tossing her from the room. If she'd questioned a partner's strategy in front of the client at her old firm, she would've risked being fired on the spot. Of course, she'd never kissed a partner at her old firm. Or told a partner she'd had a life-long crush on them. Or implied they could do more than kissing, which is where Perry had been headed that night at Birdie's, right?

Images of Stella the handsy tailor running her hands along Perry's legs filled her brain. Had Perry treated Stella to the same slow, easy smile she'd given Grace after that searing kiss at the bar? Why did she care?

Grace struggled to return to the present, to stop being distracted by Perry and her lips and inseams and the jaunty way she flaunted both of them. She had to act fast if she was going to keep Hadley on track. She was the partner at this firm and Perry was only here as a favor.

"John, any move you make right now will define not only this case," Grace said, "but how regulators view your company in the future. The allegations are broad, and the first step is to get the state to narrow them. They served us with discovery, but we can ask for discovery as well. I'm drafting requests now. Hold off on any internal actions until we have more details and can make an informed decision. I've been through these investigations before with other clients and I know what I'm doing. I understand the temptation to look for a quick and easy way out," she shot a look at Perry who merely shrugged, "but slow and steady is the way to win this type of case."

John looked at Perry like he was seeking permission to follow her advice and Perry merely hunched her shoulders. Seriously? How had a kid, barely out of law school, suddenly become the de facto authority in Grace's area of expertise? This meeting couldn't end soon enough.

Grace walked John to the lobby, partly out of courtesy and partly to keep Perry from having any alone time with him. She'd probably tell him to close his business and start planting sustainable forests instead. Once she was certain John was off the premises, she returned to the conference room, but Perry was gone. She walked to the war room, but found it empty as well. She picked up the phone on Perry's desk and buzzed Graham. "Where did Perry go?"

"Is this Ms. Maldonado?"

"Yes, Graham, it's Grace. Quit calling me Ms. Maldonado. That's my mother."

"I did not recognize your phone from this extension."

Grace sighed. "Sorry. Do you know where the young Miss Clark happens to be at this moment?"

"She had a luncheon engagement with her brother. She left mere moments ago. Would you like me to dash out to the parking lot to see if she is still on the premises?"

In the time it had taken for him to recite that long explanation, Perry was likely long gone. Besides, she didn't want to chase after Perry. It would send the wrong message. Imply she wasn't the one in control. She'd have a nice long talk with Perry later, when she'd had a chance to cool down. When her feelings about Perry the sexy kisser weren't all jumbled up with Perry the client-killer.

CHAPTER FIFTEEN

Grace read the email three times, but the message didn't change. *Before we go any further on the case, I'd like to get a second opinion. I'll give you a call soon.*

Grace threw a file folder at the wall of her office in an intense show of anger she rarely expressed. A second later, Abby appeared at her door.

"You okay?"

"Yes," Grace snarled.

Abby held her hands up, palms out. "Don't shoot, I come in peace."

Grace let out a pent up breath. No sense taking out her anger on Abby who hadn't done anything to make her mad. "Sorry, it's been hell week, and today my biggest paying client went up in flames."

Abby slipped in and shut the door behind her. She placed a finger over her lips. "Shhh, if the managing partner hears, she may fire us both."

"Very funny," Grace said. "Right now the managing partner wishes she'd never agreed to hiring an associate with no experience in commercial litigation, but if you tell Campbell I said that, I will give your parking space to Graham."

"You wouldn't dare."

Grace sighed, defeated by her true lack of power over the situation, and instantly regretting throwing Perry under the bus no matter how mad she was at her. "No, I probably wouldn't, but please don't tell. Campbell has enough going on without listening to my complaints."

"Did you really lose Hadley as a client?"

"Not officially, but I can tell he's mad. Perry ran roughshod over him during our meeting today."

Abby waved a hand dismissively. "Oh, he'll get over it. Most clients can do with a little good cop/bad cop routine. The key here is that you get to be the good cop and swoop in to save the day. Give him the weekend to cool off. Call him Monday, and I bet everything will be fine by then."

Grace considered the advice and decided Abby was probably right. Besides, she was too angry herself to try to cool Hadley down. She'd call him Monday and tell him she was pulling Perry off his case, so he didn't have to worry about any encounters with her aggressive questions again. She had the weekend to come up with a way to break the decision to Campbell.

"I know what you need," Abby said.

"What?" Grace asked, fairly certain she knew where this conversation was headed.

"Happy hour at Birdie's. I'll call Roxanne and get her to meet us there, or we can go on our own if you'd rather."

"Birdies?" Grace flashed to the last time she'd been at the bar. The dim lights, the smokey shadows, the soft beat of a ballad as Perry leaned in close and...Nope, no way was she going back there. "I think I'll pass."

Abby narrowed her eyes. "I get it. Someplace quieter. You could give the tall Swede a call and we could make it a foursome."

"Danika? Not going to happen."

"It won't if you don't invite her. Seriously, Grace, when are you going to give her a call?"

"Quit hassling me and name another place for tonight before I change my mind."

"Winebelly? Half-price bottles?"

A quiet wine bar sounded like the perfect place to relax, and she desperately needed to unwind. She still had a ton of work to do, but a glass or two of wine might relax her enough to help her get it done in the comfort of her living room. "I'm in. And invite Roxanne if you want, but two rules."

"Name them."

"No trying to fix me up with any women at the bar, and cut me off after my second glass. I've still got some work to do tonight. I need just enough wine to clear my head, but no more."

"There went all my fun."

"I live to spoil other people's dreams." She examined the words as they tumbled out of her mouth. Accurate. She'd squashed Perry's dreams by manipulating her passport delay at the embassy, and then she'd stomped on Perry's feelings last week at Birdie's. Had she always been a killjoy or was this a new skill she'd developed in her tenure as managing partner at an up-and-coming law firm?

"Come on, let's go now," Abby said, hooking arms with her. "Roxanne's meeting with a wedding planner so she'll meet us there later."

Grace walked with Abby to the lobby. "Graham, we're taking advantage of our status as partners in this illustrious business and leaving early for the day. Feel free to close up right behind us if you so desire."

"Thank you, Grace, but if it pleases you, I'd prefer to stay a bit and finish the inventory of office supplies. It is an almost insurmountable task during the fuss of the day."

Grace held back a laugh at the idea of Graham choosing paperclips over happy hour, but since it was the kind of thing she might do, she couldn't really judge. She followed Abby to the parking lot. "Roxanne's planning a wedding without you?"

"Very funny. She has a hard time telling any of her friends no when they come to her for help. What can I say, my girlfriend is the nicest person on the planet."

"You're not so bad yourself." Grace pointed at the Armada. "I'll drive. If Roxanne isn't able to meet us, I'll take you home."

It was a small thing, but having a vehicle at her disposal made her feel less out of control, and after the day she'd had, she needed all the control she could get.

The ride to Winebelly was short, and when they arrived the waiter led them to a cozy booth in the back, and Grace let her mind stray to thoughts like what a perfect venue this place was for a date. Did Perry like wine? The thought popped into her head, unbidden and she shook it away.

They ordered a bottle of red and took the first few sips before Abby launched in. "Look, I don't mean to be a nag—"

"Which is exactly what people who are about to be a nag say," Grace interjected.

"True, but I'm merely looking out for you. Danika is hot and she's clearly interested. You still have her number, right?"

Damn, Abby was persistent. "Yes, but I'm not calling again."

"Again? You called her? When? Did she call you back? What did she say?"

"Slow down," Grace said. "Yes, I called her. I asked her to brunch. We went to Magnolia last Sunday for brunch."

"And you waited this long to tell me? Have you been getting laid all week and didn't tell us? No, wait, you wouldn't be this grouchy if you were getting some."

Grace sighed. "Are you done?"

"Not even." Abby rolled her hand. "Tell me everything."

"There's not much to tell. We didn't jell."

"You didn't jell?" Abby over enunciated the words.

"That's what I said."

"What does that even mean? It sounds like code for you're not giving it a chance."

"She doesn't eat gluten."

"What?"

Grace could barely believe she'd chosen that particular nugget to defend her lack of interest in Danika, but now that she'd gone there, she went all the way. "Gluten. You know, the stuff that makes everything taste better."

"Corn tortillas, ice cream, cheese."

"Do you suddenly have food Tourette's?" Grace asked.

"So many foods without gluten."

"I guess so, but I feel pretty strongly about eliminating an entire category from my food repertoire."

Abby set her glass down and scrunched her brow. "Let me see if I'm understanding this correctly. The hot blonde with a great job asks you out, and you blow her off after one date because she has a dietary restriction?"

"It's not like that," Grace said, bracing for Abby's next question.

"Then tell me what it's like. I thought you were serious about wanting to meet someone."

Grace wanted to blurt out that she had met someone, but the someone she was completely attracted to was completely wrong for her. She needed to process her feelings, get the unrelenting distraction out of her system. She could trust Abby, right?

Neither Abby nor Campbell had ever judged her in any way, but she had a nagging feeling that whatever was going on between her and Perry might drive a wedge in her friendship with Campbell, and telling Abby could make it even worse since she'd never shared a secret with Abby or Campbell and not the other. No, she had to work out her feelings about Perry on her own, which meant she was going to bury them for now and think about something else. "I do want to meet someone, but I'm not in a hurry about it. We didn't click, it's as simple as that. You know how it is. When you know you know."

Abby nodded slowly. "You speak the truth. I knew there was something special about Roxanne from the moment I first saw her."

Grace seized on the comment to steer the conversation away from her own lack of a love life. "When is the Bride's Best Friend going to start planning her own wedding?"

Abby bit her bottom lip and avoided Grace's gaze, and Grace realized she wasn't the only one with a secret. "Have you already asked her? When? How?"

Abby shook her head. "I haven't. I don't want to horn in on Campbell's big day, but I did buy a ring, and you're officially the first person I've told." Abby pulled out her phone and scrolled through her photos. She handed the phone to Grace.

"What am I looking at here?" She enlarged the photo and gasped at the gorgeous pink gem. "Tell me that's not a natural pink diamond."

Abby grinned. "It is the genuine article."

"Abigail Keene, how in the world did you afford it? Have you been embezzling from the firm?"

"As if. No, Tommy Barclay," she said, referring to her client who owned a chain of bridal stores. "Hooked me up with his jeweler friend who cut me an amazing deal. Roxanne swoons every time she sees pink diamond engagement rings, but then she talks about how white diamonds are much more practical. Romance shouldn't be practical, should it?"

It was a loaded question, and Grace was tempted to debate the point, take Roxanne's side, and say something about how the extra money Abby had spent on the fancy pink ring would be better spent in a mutual fund, socked away for retirement. But when she replayed the thoughts in her head, even she realized they were devoid of passion. Practicality had its place, but what better time to toss off caution than when you found the one person you wanted to spend the rest of your life loving? Perry's face flashed in her mind and she could almost hear her calculating how many people could live off the proceeds of the ring, and she smiled at the thought. She pointed at the picture. "She's going to love it, and she's going to love you for noticing what she likes. But just so you know, she'd love you even without the pink ring because you're a great catch."

Abby grinned again. "Thanks, G. And the right person is out there for you. I predict she's going to show up soon. Promise me you'll keep an open mind, gluten and all."

"I promise."

An hour later, they'd polished off the bottle of wine and caught up on current events. She considered ditching the work she'd had planned for the rest of the evening and asking Abby if she wanted to order a bottle of champagne to toast her impending engagement, but before she could make the suggestion, Abby's phone pinged with a text from Roxanne.

"She's done with her client. Should I ask her to join us?"

Grace loved Roxanne, but the idea of spending Friday night as a third wheel, especially now that she held the secret of the pink ring, wasn't very appealing. "I should go. I'm pretty beat, but have her meet you here and I've got the next bottle." She pulled out her credit card and went in search of their waiter.

Thirty minutes later, she walked through the door to her house, chucked off her shoes, changed into something comfortable, and poured a finger of whiskey into one of her fancy Dutch glasses. If she was going to have to work on a Friday night, at least she was going to do it in comfort. She tucked into one of the barstools at her kitchen island and reached into her briefcase for her laptop.

Uh-oh. She pulled the bag toward her and rummaged through all the compartments, but it wasn't there. She could've sworn she'd taken it with her when she'd left the office, but she'd been so wound up, it was possible she'd forgotten. Either someone had taken it out of her car while she was at Winebelly or it was still sitting on her desk at the firm. Not knowing was eating at her. She reached for her phone, hoping Graham had been serious when he said he was working late, and she dialed the firm. She waited through the rings, about to hang up, when finally, the ringing stopped and a voice answered. "Clark, Keene, and Maldonado."

The voice was familiar, but it wasn't Graham. "Perry?"

Chapter Sixteen

G race?" Perry stared at the phone, suddenly unable to form more words. She'd been about to call Campbell to see how much longer before she showed up, but the insistent ringing of the phone on Graham's desk had compelled her to answer, and now Grace was on the other end of the line and she had no idea what to say. Judging by the silence, Grace didn't either.

"Uh, is Graham there?"

"Graham left a little while ago. Do you want me to call him?" There, she'd managed to speak two whole sentences.

"No, that's okay. I was just…I mean I think I may have left my laptop in my office, and I was going to ask him to check and see if it's there."

"I can look. Hang on." Perry set the handset down, ignoring Grace's voice telling her not to bother. She jogged back to Grace's office and spotted the laptop sitting in the center of her desk. She picked up the extension. "Guess what I'm looking at right now."

"Damn. I mean I'm glad it's there and I didn't misplace it."

"Do you need it right now?"

A second of silence and then, "No, it's fine. I was going to do some work tonight, but I'll run by and pick it up tomorrow. Thanks."

Perry stared at the phone in her hand, uncertain about what had just happened, but certain Grace had hung up on her after the longest conversation they'd had all week. She set the handset down and spotted a scrawled set of notes in Grace's handwriting on the pad next to the phone. *Ways to win Hadley back. Apology. Reduce fee. New strategy.*

Perry's gut clenched. She'd acted out during the meeting with Hadley that morning, but she hadn't said anything she hadn't meant. Had her honesty cost Grace a client? That hadn't been her goal, and she felt a surge of guilt. Was that why Grace was working on Friday night—to try to win back the favor of John Hadley? Perry might not agree with the approach, but she didn't want to be responsible for any harm to Grace's livelihood.

She couldn't repair the damage she'd done, but she could make sure Grace had what she needed to try to win Hadley back. She shoved the laptop in her backpack and fired a text off to Campbell. *Don't worry about picking me up. I've got plans. See you later.*

Next, she downloaded an app for the least vile ride share company, and walked out front, making sure the front door of the law firm locked behind her. The driver who picked her up was very chatty, but content to carry most of the conversation, which was great since she was consumed with trying to think of what she would say once she showed up on Grace's doorstep. *Here's your laptop, can we be friends again? Here's your laptop, want to go get a drink? Here's your laptop…*

Ugh. There wasn't anything to say. She'd told Grace she was interested and she knew Grace was interested too. If Grace wasn't willing to act on her feelings, there wasn't anything left to say. When the car pulled up in front of Grace's house, Perry started to tell him to keep driving, certain showing up unannounced was a terrible idea. Grace was a planner, queen of the careful maneuvers—not the kind of woman who welcomed unannounced guests.

But she was here and she had something Grace wanted. She would give her the laptop and leave. It was a small overture of peace. "Wait here," she told the driver. "I'll be right back."

She took the steps two at a time, determined to get this errand over with as quickly as possible. When she reached the door, she pressed the doorbell and waited, shifting from one foot to the other, but when Grace flung open the door, she came to attention.

"Perry?" Grace looked over her shoulder out toward the street. "What are you doing here?"

"Don't worry, I'm not staying." Perry tried not to stare at Grace's short shorts, long bare legs, and her thin cotton T-shirt—thin enough to reveal she wasn't wearing a bra. She reached into her backpack and pulled out the laptop. She handed it to Grace. "I brought you this." She backed up a step. "Well, I better get going."

Grace looked at the car and back to her. "Who drove you here?"

"Some chatty guy named Flint. He has purple hair, but he's a platinum level driver so he knows his stuff, at least that's what he told me about a dozen times. I know, I know, I said ride share was the transportation of the devil, but you sounded like you really needed your laptop, and…" Grace was staring at her like she'd lost her mind and when she replayed her words she realized she was rambling like a kid on a first date. She took another step back. "Anyway, Flint will start worrying if I don't come back soon."

"Tell Flint he's free for the night and come in and talk to me."

Perry looked back at the car and then back at Grace, trying to decipher her expression. "Are you sure?"

"Yes. See you inside."

Grace turned around and walked back into the house, leaving the door open a tiny crack. Perry stared at the crack musing that it could be a metaphor for the extent of her relationship with Grace. Big enough to see what she wanted, but too small to find a way through. If she stayed would she get a chance to see inside or was Grace going to use this opportunity to drive home her ever practical point about their respective roles and why kissing was a bad idea?

Perry looked back at the car and Flint waved. If she cut him loose, she'd be stuck here, at the mercy of Grace's mood. Of course, she could call another car, but there would be logistics, like did she stand in Grace's front yard and wait for a ride or stay inside and look out the window? Bottom line, things could get awkward, and she didn't want to feel awkward. She'd spent a week dwelling on every detail of the kiss they'd shared. She'd kissed a ton of women before, but kissing Grace had been different. The other women had been casual, fleeting—classmates in law school, various locals she'd met in her travels, and the random fellow activist, like Linda. She hadn't shared a history with any of them, not like she had with Grace. If she chose to stay and there was no kissing, could they go back to whatever they'd been before the kissing? She wasn't sure, but she was here and she might as well find out.

Grace's house was about what she expected. Everything was immaculate and organized, more of a museum feel than a home. She called out to Grace who'd apparently disappeared into its depths.

"I'm back here. In the kitchen."

Perry followed the sound of her voice, and found Grace leaning against a massive granite-topped kitchen island drinking from a glass of clear liquid. She pointed at the glass. "Gin?"

"No," Grace said, her tone brusque. "I'm working."

"I was kidding, but no one would blame you if you had a few drinks. It's Friday night after all."

"Already had two, but now I have to figure out how to clean up a mess someone made before I can enjoy the rest of my weekend."

"I'm sorry what I said caused you problems with Hadley, but I meant what I said."

"Maybe not so much with the saying everything you think. That approach may work for you in your other work, but we have to keep paying clients happy if we want to stay in business. That means having a filter and using it. We could get Hadley to see some of your points, but it's easier to do when we get him to feel like it was his idea in the first place instead of bludgeoning him over the head with criticism."

Perry had to concede Grace had a point. "I'm not real patient, in case you haven't noticed."

"Oh, I noticed," Grace said with a trace of a smile.

"Why do I feel like we're not just talking about Hadley anymore?" Perry took a step closer, emboldened by the apparent thaw in Grace's icy demeanor. She was standing about a foot from Grace, and every detail about her became larger than life Technicolor. Her dark brown eyes were deep pools of desire and her waves of hair were tousled like she'd been running her hands through it, and Perry craved the opportunity to do the same. It would be thick and soft, and she would bury her face in it, drowning in her scent.

Grace's palm on her chest, pushing her backward pulled her back to reality. She met Grace's eyes expecting to see firm resolution, but instead she looked perplexed. "What are you thinking right now?"

"That you should probably go," Grace said, her voice a whisper.

"But you don't want me to."

"It doesn't matter what I want."

Perry wanted to pull Grace into her arms and tell her what she wanted was the only thing that mattered, but she knew it was a conclusion Grace had to reach all on her own. "I want you. Does that matter?"

Grace's palm moved up from her chest to her shoulder, her finger grazing the side of Perry's neck. Perry barely held back a moan as the featherlight touch sent waves of arousal coursing through her entire body. Grace cupped her hand around the back of her neck, and now, instead of pushing she was pulling Perry toward her. Their lips were close, and the ache of almost touching took Perry's breath away. "Tell me what you want?"

Grace answered by leaning even closer, her breath labored and her eyes dark with desire.

"Do you want to keep fighting?"

Grace shook her head.

"I think we should try kissing again. If you hate it, I'll go. I swear." Perry waited, and the seconds it took for Grace to respond felt like centuries. When Grace finally nodded, she was poised and ready. She took Grace's lips between hers, lingering mere moments before pressing deeper with her tongue. Grace opened up to her as if there'd never been anything between them—age, distance, time. Every impediment fell away in favor of the thrum of desire consuming them. She ran her hands along Grace's side, up her T-shirt, moaning at the feel of her firm, round breasts. Grace's nipples peaked against the caress of her thumb, and she could feel Grace tense in her arms. "Are you okay?" she murmured against Grace's lips, praying it was.

"Okay is not the word I would use."

"Then tell me what word you would use because I'm going crazy here."

Grace grinned and reached for her hand. "Crazy, huh?"

"Certifiable." She stepped closer, her chest now pressed against Grace's. "Would you like to feel exactly how excited you make me?"

Grace tilted her head and stared into her eyes. Perry remained still for fear any sudden movement would tip the balance out of her favor.

"Yes, I would. But what about after?"

Perry's gut reaction was to say "what about it," but she knew how much it meant to Grace to be in control, and that included knowing outcomes they had no way of predicting. She gave the most honest answer she could. "I don't know, but we'll figure it out together." She raised Grace's hand to her lips and kissed her fingertips, one by one. "Do you want to figure it out together?"

Grace reached around her waist, pulled her closer, and whispered in her ear. "There are many things I want to do together."

Perry breathed deep as Grace's words conjured titillating images. "Take me to your bedroom. Please."

Grace grasped her hand and led her through the living room to a doorway on the other side. She reached in and flipped a switch and dim lights shone from the recessed fixtures on the ceiling. From the threshold, Perry could tell this room was Grace's favorite. Unlike the untouchable perfection of the other rooms she'd seen,

Grace's bedroom was approachable. Scattered magazines, tossed pillows, a fluffy comforter—simple, but telling signs. This room was where she shed her tight grip on self-control, and Perry took it as a privilege to be invited in. She let Grace lead her to the bed and she sat on the edge in front of her, waiting, ceding the first move. "Whatever you want."

"I want you to take charge."

Perry wanted to ask her to repeat the words, so surprised she was to hear the request, but she sensed Grace might withdraw if pressed. Instead she decided to go for it, certain Grace would stop her if she changed her mind. "Happy to."

She placed a hand on either side of Grace's waist and pulled her T-shirt over her head. The firm round breasts she'd felt earlier were more luscious than she could've imagined. Grace's nipples were erect, and Perry licked her lips at the sight. She traced them with her fingers, pinching gently as Grace arched into her palms, groaning with pleasure.

"That feels incredible," Grace gasped. "Don't stop."

"I have no intention of stopping," Perry said. She leaned forward and replaced her fingers with the flat of her tongue, stroking Grace's nipples in teasing turns of hard and soft, hard and soft until she whimpered in her arms. "Do you want me to stop?" Perry asked, her mouth still pressed against Grace's breast.

"Please don't."

Perry continued to lavish one breast then the other, but she dropped her hand and gently pushed Grace's shorts off her trim hips and onto the floor, excited when she felt nothing but flesh beneath. She drew a line with her finger from Grace's belly button to the apex of her sex and then curved out to her thigh, letting one finger dip into her silken and incredibly wet folds. Grace cried out and sagged against her at the touch, and Perry decided it was time they both got into the bed. Reluctantly, she eased her attention from Grace's breasts and turned her body so Grace was backed up to the bed now. She reached around her and fluffed the pillows, gently pressing Grace's back against them. "Comfortable?"

"Perfect." Grace frowned. "Except for one thing."

"Name it."

Grace reached for Perry's shirt. "Take this off." She pointed at Perry's pants. "Those too."

Perry grinned, happy to comply. She took her time shedding her clothes, making a little show of it.

"Quit being such a tease," Grace said.

"Quit being a control freak and enjoy the show." Perry held up her boxer briefs and twirled them in the air. When she let them fly, Grace grabbed her arm.

"The control freak would like the naked girl to join her in the bed."

Perry slid up close to Grace and kissed the side of her neck while she resumed touching Grace's breasts. When Grace started writhing, she reached across her and slid her naked center over Grace's, eliciting a deep groan.

"Oh, yes."

Perry repeated the move, and this time she pressed firmly against Grace's wet sex, easing open her thighs with her knees. "You're so wet," she whispered before dragging her tongue down the length of Grace's chest.

"Is that me? I thought it was you."

"The arousal is mutual. You are so incredibly hot."

"You. You are."

Perry answered by placing her hands beneath Grace's butt and nestling between her legs. The moment she dipped her tongue into Grace's sex, everything else fell away. There was only her and Grace and this moment, wherever it led. She stroked gently at first, but then with increasing pressure in response to Grace's cries, urging her on, begging her not to stop. She was in complete control, with one simple mission. She wanted to please Grace, tease her into the most explosive orgasm of her life, and moments later, when Grace shuddered in her arms, she hoped this night was one Grace would remember, no matter what happened tomorrow or the next day.

❖

Grace couldn't move, didn't want to move, decided moving was overrated. Who would move when a beautiful woman was lying in your bed, between your legs with her delicious lips a whisper away from rousing you to another orgasm?

When Perry inched her way back up to join her on the pillow, Grace took the time to appreciate every inch of her beautiful body—narrow hips, long legs, and the kind of abs that most people had to spend hours at the gym to build.

"Are you staring at me?" Perry asked.

"Maybe. Yes." Grace licked her lips. "Absolutely. Is that a problem?"

Perry tucked her arm under the pillow and drew Grace into the crook of her arm. "That is definitely not a problem."

Grace play swatted her stomach. "I knew you liked it. Exhibitionist?"

"Really? Pretty sure you were naked first."

"My clothes were ripped from me. I had no control."

Perry laughed. "Oh, baby, you have all the control, and trust me, that's a good thing."

Grace ran her tongue along the side of Perry's torso, a joking move at first, but then her lips grazed Perry's breast and elicited a soft moan. "This control thing is nice. Would you like me to stay in charge?"

"I would. I would like that very much."

Grace answered by shifting and placing her entire mouth over Perry's breast, gently drawing her nipple between her teeth and swirling her tongue around the tip. Perry gripped the sheets and arched off the bed.

"Oh my God, that feels amazing."

Grace released Perry's nipple from her mouth and stroked it with the palm of her hand. "I think you might be a little turned on."

"No doubt. I spent the last hour making love to a beautiful woman. Can you blame me for being on the edge of an orgasm?"

Making love. Grace liked the way the words sounded even if she was pretty sure Perry was only using them as a placeholder. Not that she expected anything else. This was sex, not love. The fact she'd known Perry all her life didn't change that. She felt a hand on hers, stilling her touch.

"Are you okay?"

"Sure," she said, "of course."

"Where did you go just now?"

Grace pointed at her head. "Sorry, brain never shuts off. It's not my best trait."

Perry sat up and leaned back against the pillows. "Actually, your brain is the very first part of you I was attracted to. But we can stop now if you want."

"You don't want me to..." Grace tried not to stumble over the words. "Make love to you?"

"I want you to do whatever you want." Perry shrugged like they were talking about grabbing a cup of coffee, but the way she ducked her head and avoided Grace's eyes, conveyed her desire was stronger than she was willing to let on. "You're the control freak, remember? But no pressure. I'm good."

Control freak. Excellent cover. Grace had no idea where this would lead or what it meant, and those two facts were clearly freaking her out, but she could play the part of control freak with one hand tied behind her back, and in that role she could either stop now or vow to contain whatever fallout came from this interlude between them. She looked down at Perry's body, naked, willing, ready, and knew stopping wasn't an option. "Tell you what. You're good when I say you're good."

A smile spread across Perry's face, and Grace reached for her arms, pinning them above her head with one hand. She dipped down and lightly kissed Perry's lips before turning her attention back to her small, firm breasts, taking turns with her tongue and her fingers to tease her nipples into hard points of pleasure. Perry moaned and writhed at her touch and Grace drank in the heady thrill of eliciting such a visceral response. She wanted more.

She dropped her hand lower, charting a path along Perry's sculpted stomach, winding her way down her thigh, stopping shy of the apex between her legs.

"You're making me crazy," Perry said, her breathing labored.

"Said the original crazy-maker." Grace warmed at the compliment and slid her hand between Perry's legs, trailing her fingers through her wet center, her own body throbbing at the intensity of the touch. "You feel so good."

"You're telling me." Perry arched up again to meet her touch. "I want to feel you inside. Please."

"Yes, soon." Keeping her hand between Perry's legs, she shifted position so she was on top and she kissed her way down the length of Perry's body, settling between her legs. She traced the inside of Perry's thigh with her tongue, groaning at the immediate response as Perry twitched at the lightest of touches. "You're so ready."

"Yes," Perry cried out.

Grace couldn't bear to tease her any longer. She pressed her tongue against Perry's folds and slid a finger gently inside, gasping at how quickly Perry constricted at the touch. She raised her head enough to ask, "More?"

"Oh yes."

Grace answered with two fingers, then three, easing in and out, a slow build accompanied by teasing Perry's clit with her tongue, and relishing how it became harder with each pass. As Perry bucked against her, she increased the pace, no longer able to gauge the difference between Perry's arousal and her own, and when Perry shuddered and went still, she experienced her own explosive release.

She left her hand in place and laid her head on Perry's thigh, content to stay in this spot for as long as Perry would let her.

"I've never come like that."

Grace kissed her damp skin, smiling at Perry's words and the way she trembled as she kissed her. "Like what?"

"Like someone else is totally in charge of my happiness and I'm absolutely okay with it and actually it was even better being able to completely let go."

Grace laughed and crawled back up to the top of the bed. She curled around Perry's body, craving the closeness, the intimacy of this moment. "Maybe control freaks are your thing."

Perry turned her head and captured her lips in a long, delicious kiss. "I think you may be right."

Chapter Seventeen

Perry reached for the nightstand and checked the time on her phone, surprised to see it was already six p.m. Despite the hour, Grace was snoozing gently beside her, her face a study in calm. She scrolled through the messages on her phone, mostly from Campbell, mostly wondering where she was and why she hadn't called. She set the phone down without responding, rolled out of Grace's bed, and started looking for the clothes she'd worn when she'd shown up last night.

She didn't want to go, but after breaking her promise to spend the day with Campbell, she figured she should at least show up for dinner with her and Wynne tonight. Grace reached for her leg as she walked by, and Perry smiled down at her. She'd never seen Grace this relaxed, this uninhibited. She was naked except for the fold of sheet barely covering her thigh. "Hello, you."

"Hello, yourself. Are you leaving?"

Perry spotted her pants lying a few feet away and she tugged them on, and then leaned down to kiss Grace on the forehead. "I promised Campbell I'd have dinner with her and Wynne. Do you secretly want me to stay?"

"I do want you to stay, but there's no secret about it."

Grace's honesty warmed her soul. "I'll text Campbell and tell her I can't make it."

Grace shifted under her and placed a hand on her chest. "No, you won't. I got you yesterday, it's her turn."

"Apples and oranges."

"Am I the apple or the orange?"

Perry nuzzled against Grace's shoulder, leaving a trail of kisses along the side of her neck, and finishing by nibbling her ear. "You're a mango. More complex than an apple or orange. Fragrant, juicy—"

Grace shook her head. "Okay, okay, your career as a poet has just ended. There will be no more talk of fruit. But seriously, you should go. You haven't gotten to spend much time with Campbell, and since I'm already making plans to monopolize you the rest of the week, you should take advantage of this opportunity. Besides, I may need a little time to recover. I don't think I've ever had sex for twelve hours solid without a break."

Perry smiled and kissed her again. "I'm all about setting records. Next time, let's go for twenty-four."

Less than an hour later, Flint, who'd been excited to be requested again, dropped Perry off at Campbell's house. She'd hated leaving Grace, gorgeous, naked, insatiable Grace, but she felt good about her decision to keep her word and join Campbell and Wynne for dinner. She could do commitment in small doses and it didn't hurt that keeping this one had scored her bonus points with Grace.

She put her key in the lock of Campbell's house, but it swung open before she could turn the knob. Campbell stood on the other side and she didn't look happy.

"Where have you been?"

And just like that, the glow she'd been feeling after her night with Grace faded. Perry pushed past Campbell to walk into the house, her guard up at the edge in Campbell's voice. "Nice to see you too, sis."

"Sorry, but I have a right to be concerned. You've been MIA almost twenty-four hours."

"So, you've mentioned. Twice. In case you forgot, I am an adult. Besides, I texted you to say I wasn't going to be home. I'm sorry I missed today, but since you'd planned all that stuff to make me feel better, I thought you'd be relieved to know I found my own way out of my funk."

"You chose to spend the day with some girl you met at the bar instead of your own sister who hasn't gotten to spend one-on-one time with you in years, and that's supposed to make me feel better?"

Perry studied Campbell's face. She'd grown used to Campbell playing parent, but this was something else. Campbell felt genuinely dissed. "Hey, I'm sorry. I guess I didn't think you really wanted to do all that stuff. That you were just doing it for me, and since I was…you know, I figured I was letting you off the hook."

"I've barely seen you. Maybe next time choose me instead of a stranger." Campbell waved toward the kitchen. "Come on, dinner's almost ready."

Campbell hadn't raised her voice, but her even keel didn't hide the fact she was annoyed, and now Perry was annoyed too at Campbell's implication she'd put a stranger before her own family. Sure, she hadn't been around much, but she still loved Campbell and Justin as much as she'd loved their parents. And that was the problem. Would Campbell ever stop trying to be Mom, so they could be sisters instead? Sisters who shared important things without fear of judgment. For years, she'd chafed at Campbell's attempts to micromanage her life, and her annoyance bubbled to the surface. "I wasn't with a stranger."

Campbell stopped and turned around. "What?"

"I wasn't with a stranger. I was with Grace." Perry stared at her, daring her to speak, but Campbell stood in place, silent except for the glower emanating from her eyes. Perry decided to go all in. "That's right, Grace. Your best friend, the managing partner of your law firm. An amazing woman by anyone's standards. You want to tell me again how I don't make responsible choices?"

Campbell walked toward her, and Perry resisted backing away at her ominous approach. "You're telling me that you spent the last twenty-four hours with Grace? At her house?"

"Yes. And we weren't playing Scrabble, if that's your next question."

"I don't believe you."

"Call her and ask." Perry prayed she wouldn't. She'd known, on some level, Campbell would be upset that she'd slept with Grace, but she hadn't expected nuclear level anger. "Why are you mad?"

Campbell shook her head. "Mad? You think I'm mad? Grace is my best friend. You had a weekend of fun, got what you wanted, and as soon as your passport comes in, you're going to leave, right?"

Perry averted her eyes, unable to stand Campbell's steely gaze. "That's the plan."

"And where does that leave Grace?"

"What are you talking about?"

"I'm talking about my best friend, who apparently blew off a chance to date a woman her own age with a great job for a fling. Does she know it was a fling? Does she understand you're out of here as soon as you get the chance?"

"She's not a child, Campbell. You can treat me like a kid all you want, but Grace is a grown woman who can make her own decisions. She was as into it as I was."

Campbell put her hands over her ears. "Stop. I don't want to hear it."

"Then you shouldn't have brought it up." She took her tone down a notch, hoping to diffuse the situation. "We're consenting adults. Grace knows I'm not staying in Austin. We had fun and that's all it was." As she spoke the words, a nagging voice within called them into question, but she batted it away, forging ahead. "Once I'm gone, she can resume whatever with that leggy blonde. It's all good."

She watched Campbell for some sign she was getting through, but Campbell's frown appeared to be permanent. There was no pleasing her, no matter what she did or didn't do. The realization fueled her anger. "And by the way, if you wanted me to stand up for you at your wedding, you could've asked." Campbell looked shocked at the remark, but Perry attributed it to the abrupt change in subject.

"I wanted to surprise you. With the tux. Stella came to the office, right?"

Perry knew this was the point in the argument where she was supposed to say thank you and tell Campbell she was sorry for bristling under her control, but now that her happy afterglow had been extinguished, she wasn't in the mood to make nice. "Yes. Did you bother telling your best friend you plan to have me be the maid of honor or whatever?"

"Yes, Grace knows I planned to ask you. Does she know you might not even show up?"

"Grace knows me better than you do."

"Has she seen this side of you yet? The one that runs away at the first sign of an emotional connection to anything?"

That's it. She was done. She'd promised, over and over, that she'd be there for the wedding, but apparently Campbell didn't believe her, and it was about to become a self-fulfilling prophecy. Campbell wasn't going to be satisfied with anything she said or did. At least not until she quit her job with Lawyers for Change and moved back to Austin. Well, if Campbell wanted her to make a move, she was ready. "Tell Wynne I'm sorry I couldn't make it for dinner."

"What? Where are you going?"

"Upstairs to get my stuff. I'm going to stay at Justin's for a while." She started up the stairs.

"Perry, don't go. We can work this out."

"Maybe, but not right now. I need some space."

Campbell stared at her for a moment, and when she spoke her voice was even, but Perry could hear the frustration beneath her words. "Fine, but I think you better not come back to the office for now."

Perry instantly thought of a dozen responses. No big deal that she was effectively being fired from a job Campbell had made up to keep her from doing what she really loved. What did Campbell think she was accomplishing by this move? If she and Grace wanted to date each other, barring her from the office wasn't going to stop that.

She rolled that last thought around in her head for a moment. She wasn't dating Grace. Nope. She'd just told Campbell what she had with Grace was casual, but now she wasn't certain that was true. Was it a matter of wanting something she was told she couldn't have or were the feelings she'd had when she and Grace made love for real?

She couldn't think about this now. She needed to spend some time alone and clear her head. "Fine." It wasn't fine.

Thirty minutes later, she was in the back seat of Flint's car, grateful he'd still been in the neighborhood and grateful his constant stream of chatter managed to drown out the barrage of thoughts about Grace and Campbell and the future. The thoughts, she could handle, but the feelings that came with them made her want to run fast and far away.

Chapter Eighteen

Grace sensed something was wrong the minute she walked into the office on Monday morning. Graham, who usually greeted her with an overly formal prediction of the state of the world, abruptly ended the call he was on and simply said, "Conference room. Campbell and Abby are waiting."

"I didn't see a meeting on my calendar," she said, hoping he could give her a heads-up as to what was going on. "New client?"

Graham hunched his shoulders. "I am merely the messenger."

She stared at him for a moment, and although she was certain he knew more, he didn't cave under her gaze. "Tell them I'll be there in a minute."

She stopped in her office and unpacked her bag, setting her laptop on the center of her desk. The laptop she'd insisted she had to have at home with her this weekend had been barely used. After Perry had left Saturday night, she'd been too consumed with after sex haze to manage to do any work, and yesterday had been more of the same. Several times, she'd pulled out her phone, planning to text Perry and invite her back over. If she wasn't going to get any work done, she may as well play, but she stopped short almost every time. She didn't like to ask questions when she wasn't sure of the answers, and no matter how intimate their time together had been, they hadn't touched on the topic of what would happen next beyond a simple "see you later."

Finally, right before she went to bed last night, she'd texted a simple *Had a great time with you yesterday* and set her phone down, vowing not to stalk her message app for a response. An hour later, her phone buzzed on the nightstand and she scooped it up, quickly scrolling to find two simple words. *Me too.*

That was it. No, let's do it again. It was the best night of my life. Being with you makes me want to reconsider leaving town. Had she really expected more?

She had, and she could kick herself for doing so. Perry had been clear about her intentions from the beginning. Her stay in Austin was temporary, and she wouldn't even be here had Grace not convinced her to return. When it came to the attraction between them, Perry had never mentioned anything more than wanting to live in the moment. Grace replayed their exchange for the hundredth time since Perry's text: *What about after? I don't know, but we'll figure it out together.* Well, where was the together part?

She shook her head. Enough. Enough dwelling on whether she'd made a huge mistake. Enough wondering why something that felt so good could leave her feeling positively wrecked. She had to get her act together because Campbell and Abby were waiting and she knew in her gut something serious was going on, and they were probably looking to her, as the managing partner, to offer a solution. She stood up straight, assumed her ready for trial face, and strode to the conference room.

The first thing she noticed when she entered the room was that there were no donuts, signaling the level of serious was several notches higher than she'd thought. "Sorry, I'm late, but I didn't get a message about a meeting this morning." She slid into her seat at the head of the table. "What's up?"

Neither Campbell nor Abby responded, and Abby seemed to be trying to find a particular spot on the wall to focus her attention. "Does someone want to tell me what's going on? Did we lose a big client?" Her gut clenched as she wondered if Hadley had contacted one of them to complain about last week's meeting. "Was it Hadley?"

Campbell looked at her with a puzzled expression. "What are you talking about?"

Okay, it wasn't Hadley. Could it be Leaderboard? "Did Brax fire us?"

Abby chose that moment to stop looking at the wall. Her head shake was subtle, but not so much with the way she cut her eyes toward Campbell in an over-exaggerated telegraph. Grace wasn't sure how to interpret the maneuver, but she didn't have time to be relieved they hadn't lost their most lucrative client before Campbell spoke.

"Perry quit."

Grace absorbed the stinging blow and struggled to keep her voice calm. "When?"

"Saturday night when she came home after spending the night with you."

Boom. Grace returned Campbell's glare. She got that Campbell was mad. She'd expected that, but the fact she'd been stewing about it since Saturday without reaching out to her? That wasn't how their friendship worked. They fought, sure, by hashing out their disagreements, not by keeping secrets and letting them fester. "You're saying she walked into your house and quit this job. Just like that."

"Oh, no. There was more, but I'm pretty sure you know the rest."

Grace didn't bother trying to hide her own anger in response. "All I know is that Perry was in a good mood when she left my house and she didn't say anything about quitting."

Abby stood and made a time-out motion. "Let's start over before this gets out of hand. Okay?"

Grace stared at Campbell before nodding her assent. She didn't want to fight with her, and she'd anticipated there would be fallout from sleeping with Perry, but she wasn't prepared to concede she'd done anything wrong. She and Perry were both adults. If they wanted to sleep together, that was their choice and it shouldn't matter who either one of them were related to. But it did, and behind Campbell's anger she could see hurt, and it pained her to know she'd caused it.

"All right," Abby said. "Campbell, did Perry really quit?"

Campbell sighed. "Not exactly. I may have told her not to come back to the office. It's possible she thinks she was fired."

"What did you do that for?" Grace asked, not bothering to temper her voice.

Abby waved a finger at her. "Hang on. I promise I'll get to you. Campbell, what did you do that for?"

"I don't know. It seemed like the right thing to do at the time. She'd come home from spending the weekend with Grace."

"One night," Grace interjected.

"Whatever. We had words, she packed her stuff and said she was going to Justin's, and I reacted. It's possible I overreacted. I don't know. Obviously, something's been going on between them for a while. I sensed it, but clearly they were keeping it a secret."

Abby held up a hand. "Hang on. When it comes to keeping relationships secret, I don't think either one of us has room to talk. You were sleeping with Wynne when she was competing for our business, and Roxanne and I kept seeing each other even though she was trying to put Barclay's out of business."

"Exactly," Grace said. "And come on, Campbell, you fired your sister for sleeping with your best friend. What's that about?" She paused and a nagging feeling crept in. "Do you think I'm not good enough for your sister?"

"What? That doesn't even make sense. She's the one I fired, not you."

"Well, you can't fire me because I'm your law partner."

"I thought you'd be grateful she's not here at the office."

Grace looked at Abby. "Are you hearing this nonsense?"

Campbell raised her hands in surrender. "Okay, I told her not to come back to the office because I was mad at her. She'd packed her things and was leaving the house, running away like she always does whenever there are important things to discuss or whenever she's faced with feeling anything. I said it to get a reaction. I half expected her to show up anyway out of pure stubbornness, but Justin said she was still in bed when he left for work this morning. Frankly, Grace, I did think you'd be relieved not to have to deal with the awkwardness."

Grace stood and started pacing in an attempt to digest Campbell's words without blowing up at her. When she replayed the part about awkwardness, she couldn't keep silent. "You thought I'd be relieved? Do you think I'm incapable of dealing with a little awkwardness with another woman? Especially a woman who makes me feel alive, who makes me laugh? A woman who gave me the best night of my life? It wasn't your decision to make. Whatever there is between me and Perry, it's for us to decide, and when it comes to what happens in this office, we all get an equal say."

She stopped pacing and slumped back in her chair. Abby reached out and clasped her arm in a show of solidarity. The three of them had achieved a wonderful balance over the years, each playing to their strengths in both business and friendship. Sure, they'd had minor disagreements in the time they'd been friends, but this? This was a bigger mess than any they'd faced before. She'd known better than to let anything develop between her and Perry, no matter how strong the attraction. She'd disrupted the balance, and for what? Perry wasn't even around, so she'd sacrificed her friendship for nothing.

"The best night of your life?"

Grace looked up and met Campbell's eyes. They were questioning, but kind and concerned, like she really wanted to know the truth. "Yes. I've never felt this way before. And..." she stopped, uncertain about how much was appropriate to say. "This is hard. I don't know if I'm talking to my friend Campbell or Perry's sister."

Campbell smiled. "I'm not sure how we separate the two, but try friend first."

Grace took a deep breath and slowly exhaled. She stared at her hands as she spoke. "I've never felt like this before. I've spent my life being the responsible one, the one who put work before pleasure because that's how you stay safe and sane, but when I'm with Perry, she brings out a side of me I didn't even know existed. I want to have fun and be adventurous. I want to explore markets, and ride bikes through traffic, and dance until the bar shuts down, and I want to do those things with her." She looked up, catching Abby's understanding smile before turning to face Campbell.

"You've fallen in love with her."

"Love? No." Grace glanced back at Abby. "Come on, help me out here."

"Sounds like love to me," Abby said, exchanging a knowing look with Campbell.

"You two don't know what you're talking about."

"Actually," Abby said, "We kind of do." She pointed at Campbell. "This one's getting married shortly, and...and I'm head over heels for Roxanne."

Grace play punched Abby in the arm, happy to have found a way to deflect the attention from her predicament. "You're not going to keep it a secret forever, you may as well go ahead and tell her."

"Tell me what?" Campbell asked.

"Do it or I will," Grace said.

"Fine," Abby said. "I didn't want to detract from your big day, but I bought a ring."

"OMG, let me see it," Campbell said.

Abby pulled the picture up on her phone, and Campbell oohed and aahed, while Grace watched. She'd always known she wanted what they had—someone she could share her life with, who she loved and who loved her back in equal measure. She'd planned her life carefully to prepare for finding that person, starting with establishing her career, achieving financial independence, and owning a home where she could raise a family, but in the process of checking all the boxes, she'd missed the one thing her friends hadn't—the passion part. The I don't care if it's practical, the way you make me feel and the need to be with you is so strong, nothing else matters. Suddenly, she wanted the attention back on her because she needed her friends right now. She cleared her throat, exaggerating the sound. Abby put her phone facedown on the table, and she and Campbell made a show of sitting at attention.

"What if I *was* in love with Perry?" She gave Campbell a pointed look. "It's hopeless, right? She's too young, and she doesn't want to live in Austin, and she doesn't feel that way about me." She paused to take inventory, make sure she'd listed all the reasons why it wouldn't work, when Campbell reached across the table and took her hand. "What?"

"I'm sorry. Earlier, when you asked me if I thought you weren't good enough for my sister? Well, the truth is there is no one better, and there's no one I'd rather have as a sister-in-law."

"I hear a 'but' coming," Grace said, bracing for the other shoe.

"It's not about you. I love Perry, but I don't know if she'll ever be willing to settle down, and maybe never here in Austin. I want her to, and if it was with you, I could wish nothing better for you both."

"You should tell her how you feel," Abby said. "She might stay if she knows you're in love with her."

"But what if she doesn't?"

"Then you have us." Abby reached for her other hand and Campbell nodded. "And there'll be someone else one day. You're a catch, Grace Maldonado."

Grace gripped their hands tightly. She was lucky to have such good friends. With their support she might be able to find the courage to tell Perry how she felt because that stuff Abby said about there being someone else was crap. She knew Perry was the only one for her.

CHAPTER NINETEEN

Perry heard the whir of the garage door and braced for Justin to walk in and find her in the exact same position she'd been when he'd left for work that morning. Except for a couple of trips to the kitchen for water, she'd been parked on the couch for the second day in a row. She wasn't proud of her lethargy, but she seemed unable to summon the energy to do anything following her fight with Campbell. Several times she'd picked up her phone to reach out to Grace, but stopped, finally understanding why it was a problem to get involved with her sister's best friend. If Grace agreed Campbell was being unreasonable, where would that leave their friendship? And if Grace sided with Campbell, then they'd never work out.

But they wouldn't work out anyway because Grace was firmly rooted here in Austin with her nice house and her successful law firm, representing the kind of clients who fired lawyers who pointed out their faults. Flirtation and fooling around had been fun, but they could not be more different, and she couldn't see a way to make a relationship between them work without either one of them compromising who they were. Best to let the memories of her time with Grace, from London to last weekend, stay fixed in her mind, exactly as they were instead of ruining them with inevitable clashes about the type of lives they would lead.

As the door from the garage opened, she sat up straight and attempted to feign productivity by arranging the magazines on the coffee table into a neat stack. Justin shook his head when he saw her.

"You can quit pretending," he said. "I can tell you've been moping around all day. Again."

"I'm not moping."

"Yes, you are. Any chance you want to tell me what's got you down?"

"I don't know."

"I think you do."

She sighed. Justin was rarely persistent—not like Campbell—but he deserved some answers considering she'd basically moved in with no notice. "I'm agitated."

"Oh, I could've told you that."

"I slept with Grace." She dropped the bomb and waited for it to explode, but Justin merely nodded.

"Okay. You wanted that, right? I'm guessing she decided the kissing was no longer a mistake."

"Very funny. Yes, she came around to my way of thinking. I'm very persuasive."

"Yet, here you are all agitated and mopey."

"Campbell found out and she got mad. I guess I'm not good enough for her friends. She told me not to come back to the office, and she's probably already talked to Grace, and now things are complicated."

Justin sat down in the chair across from her. "I'm trying to remember a time when you let Campbell's opinion determine your course of action."

"Okay, but—"

"And since when does complicated scare you off?"

He was right in general, but the situation with Grace was a different level of complication. "I'm not scared."

"It's okay if you are. You'd be crazy not to be. Look, I know you travel all over the world and fight legal battles in dangerous situations, but sometimes it takes more courage to face the fears inside than the ones the world throws at you. You can stay in one place if you want, get attached to people. What happened to Mom and Dad can't define your life. If you let it, you'll never have the life they would've wanted for you, for us. They had each other and a family they loved up until the moment they died. Don't trade away your chance at having the same thing for fear you might lose it one day."

Perry sat with his words, letting the truth of them seep in. He was right, but him being right didn't automatically erase her trepidation. "I hear you."

"Good." He stood. "Now, go take a shower and get dressed. We're going out to dinner."

She wanted to snuggle back into the cozy couch and shut out the world for a bit longer, but she kind of owed him the courtesy of accepting the invite considering his patience with her malaise. "Fine, but it better not be someplace dressy because I only have one clean outfit and it's super casual."

"No worries, it's come as you are."

An hour later, when Justin pulled up in front of Campbell's house, Perry knew she'd been duped. "Come on, bro. You can't be serious."

"I am. I love you both and I need you to make up. You don't have to agree on everything. You don't have to go back to work at the firm, you don't have to stay in town, but I need my family to get along. Can you do this for me?"

"When you put it that way, I guess so." Perry opened her door. "Come on, let's get this over with." She walked to Campbell's front door, surprised to find that her sense of dread dissipated with each step. She didn't want dissension any more than Justin did. If she could fix things between her and Campbell, would that pave the way for her to explore something more with Grace?

The door swung open as she approached, and Campbell walked out to meet her. Perry glanced over her shoulder, but Justin was hanging back, likely to give them time to talk. Campbell made the first move. "I'm glad you came. Wynne's making dinner, and she'd really like it if you stayed."

"Well, as long as it's Wynne cooking and not you." Perry smiled, hoping her attempt at levity didn't fall flat.

Campbell returned the smile and led the way inside to the living room. "I'm sorry I blew up at you," she said. "I think the stress of trying to balance this trial and the wedding is getting to me."

Perry appreciated the overture, but she knew they needed to talk about the real reason they'd fought or it would eat away at their relationship until it was resolved. "I'm sorry too. I hate it when we fight, but you and I both know this wasn't because of the trial or the wedding."

Campbell hung her head. "I know. Believe me, I got an earful from Grace."

"You talked to Grace?"

"Of course I did. She's my best friend, we run a business together. But, Perry, you're my sister and I love you. I don't know how whatever is happening between you two is going to play out, but I support whatever you both decide."

It felt strange knowing Campbell and Grace had talked about her that way, but Perry supposed she should've expected the lines would blur if she and Grace were anything more than friends.

"In fact, I invited her over too. I thought we could all clear the air and if you two want to talk, this would be a good neutral ground to do it."

Uh-oh, this was beginning to feel like a setup. Was Campbell trying to use Grace like she had in London, except instead of trying to lure her back to Austin, her goal now was keeping her here?

She didn't have time to think it through further before she heard Grace's voice at the door. A moment later, she rounded the corner of the living room with Justin right behind her. Seeing Grace again outside the cocoon of her bedroom felt surreal, and for a moment everything in the room faded away, leaving only her and Grace, eyes locked. She wanted to go to her. Kiss her soft lips.

Wrap her up in her arms. Whisper in her ear and tell her how much she'd missed her in the forty-eight hours they'd been apart.

Justin's voice broke into her reverie. "Campbell, the mailman came while I was standing out there. Hey, Perry, this one's for you."

She tore her gaze from Grace and stared at the envelope in his hand, instantly taking in the official seal. Could it be? Already? She grabbed the envelope, tore it open, and palmed the navy booklet that fell into her hand. She thumbed through the brand-new, unstamped pages, full of promise and possibility, but the excitement she'd expected to feel fell flat.

"It's your passport. That was fast."

Perry looked up at Grace who was standing beside her, and the irony struck hard. Grace was the reason her passport had come so quickly and now Grace was the reason she didn't need it anymore.

Wait. Had she just decided not to leave? Was she ready to make that leap? Did Grace even want her to stay? Perry looked around and noticed everyone else had scattered, leaving the two of them alone in the room. "It was fast. Maybe too fast."

"I thought it was what you wanted."

"I want a lot of things, but they're all jumbled up right now."

"John Hadley called today."

Seriously, Perry was standing here trying to come up with the right words to tell Grace she was in love with her, and Grace wanted to talk about work? Was that the reason she'd shown up at Campbell's? "Did he tell you to fire me?"

"Not even close. In fact, he called to talk to you."

Perry raised an eyebrow.

"It's true, ask Graham. Of course, I intercepted the call as any good control freak would. Do you want to know what he had to say?"

Perry didn't care what John Hadley had to say about anything because she had stuff of her own to say. Stuff that was way more important than defenses to illegal dumping and ways to circumvent environmental regulations. But Grace seemed intent on telling her, which she should probably take as a sign she'd read the signals wrong. Grace was more interested in her job than anything else, and maybe she should take her lead and call Tom and let him know she was free to travel anywhere in the world.

"Are you listening to me?" Grace asked.

Perry sighed. "John Hadley. Called about me. Go on, tell me how I lost you a client."

"But you didn't." Grace grinned. "He called to offer you a job. The arrogant jerk wanted to hire you right out from under us. He took your advice about charitable causes, but he wants to go one better. He's forming a foundation to address environmental issues from the hill country to the coast, and he wants to talk to you about running it. He was impressed by your, and I quote, 'willingness to speak truth to power.'"

Perry's head spun. "You're joking."

"Not a joke. He's for real."

"I don't have any experience running a foundation."

"He likes your passion and he has enough money to get you a staff that can handle the day-to-day. He wants you to be the face of the foundation, the fundraiser. I told him he couldn't have picked a better candidate, but you might have other plans."

Perry sunk onto the couch. Talk about big commitments. Her brain whirred at the possibilities, the opportunities a job like the one Hadley was offering would allow her to make a significant impact in the world. So why was she more disappointed than excited? "Is this why you came here tonight? To tell me about Hadley's offer?"

Grace sat beside her. "No. I didn't even know about it when I decided to come."

"Okay." Perry wasn't sure what to ask, where to start.

"I have an offer of a different sort."

"A job offer?"

Grace shook her head. "But I am looking for someone with your kind of passion."

Perry's heart beat faster. This was the moment she'd been waiting for. The moment she feared, with all Grace's talk of Hadley and his offer, had passed her by. Determined not to let the opportunity slip away, she blurted out the words she'd been practicing in her head. Words she'd never spoken out loud, but she'd written in the spiral notebooks she used to carry around when she was a kid, framed with a heart and cupid's arrow. "I love you, Grace Maldonado."

She waited, holding her breath, hoping her fantasy would come true, but she didn't have to wait long. Grace took both her hands in hers and gazed into her eyes. "I love you too, Perry Clark. And you can take the job with Hadley or tell him to shove it. I don't care either way because I want to build a life with you, and we'll work it out no matter what."

CHAPTER TWENTY

"Wake up, sleepyhead."

Grace slowly opened her eyes, squinting as they adjusted to the light. Perry was standing next to the bed, wearing a towel around her waist and nothing else, and she was holding a tray. Grace stretched her arms above her head. "This is the perfect way to wake up on a Saturday morning. Or any morning." She reached over and tugged at the towel. "Except you're wearing too many clothes."

Perry swatted her hand away and set the tray on the nightstand. "Quit trying to undress the help and have some coffee. We have a big day ahead."

Grace propped up on the pillows and took the mug Perry handed to her. "You're spoiling me."

"It's all part of the package, ma'am." Perry mimed writing in a notepad like she was taking an order. "Coffee, light cream. Young female companion, light clothing. Delivered fresh each morning." She bent down. "With a kiss."

Grace took Perry's lips between her own and savored the silky soft touch. For the past two weeks, she'd gone to bed with Perry by her side and woken to this same ritual, and it was still fresh and new and joyful. She deepened the kiss, and when Perry's eyes shuttered and she could tell she was in the haze of arousal, she reached behind her and ripped the towel away.

"You got me," Perry said, sounding happy about it.

"I kind of think you let me." Grace ran a finger up Perry's thigh. "Are you sure we don't have time for you to crawl back in bed and let me have my way with you?"

"Not until the brides leave for their honeymoon." Perry backed just out of reach. "Until then, we're team maid of honor. I hung our clothes and shoes by the front door, and I'm going to pack some snacks. Enjoy your coffee. It's going to be a long day, but we've got this."

Perry started to walk away, but Grace reached for her and she returned to her side. "You're pretty incredible. Kiss me one more time and I swear I'll leave you alone until our bridal party duties are done for the day, or at least until after you give your toast at the reception. I can't make any promises about what will happen once the champagne starts flowing."

"Deal." Perry bent and kissed her again, a quick, light kiss. The kind they'd exchanged dozens of times since Perry had moved in. The kind of kiss that said I want you to know there will be more where that came from. Grace watched her leave the room, enjoying the sight of her tight round butt wrapped in a towel. Morning coffee had never tasted so good.

An hour later, she drove while Perry navigated the way to Moonlight Ranch. Abby's mom had gotten married here last year, and Campbell had fallen in love with the setting. The massive property boasted several different venues, all fully customizable, and Campbell and Wynne had selected a canopy near the edge of a bluff for their ceremony and the large pavilion strung with shiny, twinkling stars nearby for the reception. They'd planned a full day of events, including brunch for their closest friends and family, and Kate's Donuts was already on hand preparing trays of fresh-made deliciousness.

Grace pulled the car to a stop in the parking lot and reached for Perry's hand. "Two things."

"Name them."

"I am fully dedicated to Campbell's happiness today, and I know that we're probably going to both be running in different directions to make sure everything goes smoothly, but I want you to know that wherever you are today, I'll be thinking of you and wishing you were by my side."

Perry grinned. "I like the sound of thing one. What's thing two?"

Grace tugged her closer. "When Campbell and Wynne get back from their honeymoon, let's take a trip of our own. Wherever you want to go. As long as there are no thirty-story Ferris wheels in my future."

"I seem to recall you hanging on tight during that particular ride."

"Don't worry, I'll hang on tight no matter what as long as you'll let me. I have a lot more to lose now."

"A trip it is." Perry kissed her, lingering over her lips like she was reconsidering her plans for the day before she eased away. "I'll be thinking about you all day. Someday, this will be us."

Grace watched her face carefully for any sign she was joking around, but the intensity of Perry's gaze told her she was completely serious. Before she could respond, Perry was out of her seat. "Let's go," she said as she jumped down from the SUV.

Perry's words lingered with her all day, and the more she tried them on for size, the more she liked the way they fit. Perry had started working with Hadley to put together the foundation, and Grace had watched carefully, on the lookout for any signs Perry was bored with the work or unsettled about remaining in Austin. On the contrary, she seemed to be in her element, full of ideas of how Hadley could partner with other foundations across the country and even globally to have a wider reach.

Later in the day, Grace and Abby led Campbell to the dressing room and helped her get ready. "Who's with Wynne?" Grace asked. "Does she need anything?"

Campbell shot her a look. "Don't you dare abandon me. Her best friend, Seth, is the best man, and Roxanne's checking on her."

"I checked on her too," Perry said as she strode into the room, looking stunning in her midnight blue tux, tailored perfectly to her body. "She's fine."

"There's a lot of fine going around," Abby said. "Check out this tux."

Campbell feigned shock. "That's my little sister you're talking about."

"And my girlfriend," Grace said, taking Perry's arm. "But you don't hear me complaining about Abby's assessment." She ran her hands down Perry's lapels. "So much fine."

"Hey, over here," Campbell called out, waving her hands. "Get your own wedding. You're supposed to be doting on me on my special day."

Abby and Grace let out a collective groan at the words "special day" and then they all burst into laughter, except Perry. "What's so funny?" she asked.

"You had to be there," Abby said.

"All right then." Perry checked her phone. "I'm going to do one last lap around the pavilion. Last time I checked, Braxton Meadows was eating all the donuts. I'll be back in a bit."

Grace followed her to the door, Campbell's joking words, "get your own wedding," playing on a loop in her head. She adjusted Perry's tie and leaned in to give her a kiss before whispering, "I heard you before." At Perry's puzzled look, she added. "In the car. When you said, 'someday this will be us.'"

Perry smiled. "You *are* the marrying kind, aren't you?"

"When the right woman comes along, I'm asking." Grace said.

"And how will you know she's the right woman?"

Grace reached for Perry's hand and held it to her heart. "She'll be smart, and kind, and funny, romantic, and sexy. And I suspect she'll look a lot like you."

"I suspect she'll say yes the minute you ask."

"I can't wait to find out."

THE END

About the Author

Carsen Taite is a recovering lawyer who prefers writing fiction to practicing law because she has more control of the outcome. She believes that lawyers make great lovers, which is why she includes so many of them in her novels. She is the award-winning author of over twenty-five novels of romance and romantic intrigue, including the Luca Bennett Bounty Hunter series, the Lone Star Law series, and the Legal Affairs romances.

Books Available from Bold Strokes Books

Best Practice by Carsen Taite. When attorney Grace Maldonado agrees to mentor her best friend's little sister, she's prepared to confront Perry's rebellious nature, but she isn't prepared to fall in love. Legal Affairs: one law firm, three best friends, three chances to fall in love. (978-1-63555-361-1)

Home by Kris Bryant. Natalie and Sarah discover that anything is possible when love takes the long way home. (978-1-63555-853-1)

Keeper by Sydney Quinne. With a new charge under her reluctant wing—feisty, highly intelligent math wizard Isabelle Templeton—Keeper Andy Bouchard has to prevent a murder or die trying. (978-1-63555-852-4)

One More Chance by Ali Vali. Harry Bastantes planned a future with Desi Thompson until the day Desi disappeared without a word, only to walk back into her life sixteen years later. (978-1-63555-536-3)

Renegade's War by Gun Brooke. Freedom fighter Aurelia DeCallum regrets saving the woman called Blue. She fears it will jeopardize her mission, and secretly, Blue might end up breaking Aurelia's heart. (978-1-63555-484-7)

The Other Women by Erin Zak. What happens in Vegas should stay in Vegas, but what do you do when the love you find in Vegas changes your life forever? (978-1-63555-741-1)

The Sea Within by Missouri Vaun. Time is running out for Dr. Elle Graham to convince Captain Jackson Drake that the only thing that can save future Earth resides in the past, and rescue her broken heart in the process. (978-1-63555-568-4)

To Sleep With Reindeer by Justine Saracen. In Norway under Nazi occupation, Marrit, an Indigenous woman; and Kirsten, a Norwegian resister, join forces to stop the development of an atomic weapon. (978-1-63555-735-0)

Twice Shy by Aurora Rey. Having an ex with benefits isn't all it's cracked up to be. Will Amanda Russo learn that lesson in time to take a chance on love with Quinn Sullivan? (978-1-63555-737-4)

Z-Town by Eden Darry. Forced to work together to stay alive, Meg and Lane must find the centuries-old treasure before the zombies find them first. (978-1-63555-743-5)

Bet Against Me by Fiona Riley. In the high stakes luxury real estate market, everything has a price, and as rival Realtors Trina Lee and Kendall Yates find out, that means their hearts and souls, too. (978-1-63555-729-9)

Broken Reign by Sam Ledel. Together on an epic journey in search of a mysterious cure, a princess and a village outcast must overcome life-threatening challenges and their own prejudice if they want to survive. (978-1-63555-739-8)

Just One Taste by CJ Birch. For Lauren, it only took one taste to start trusting in love again. (978-1-63555-772-5)

Lady of Stone by Barbara Ann Wright. Sparks fly as a magical emergency forces a noble embarrassed by her ability to submit to a low-born teacher who resents everything about her. (978-1-63555-607-0)

Last Resort by Angie Williams. Katie and Rhys are about to find out what happens when you meet the girl of your dreams but you aren't looking for a happily ever after. (978-1-63555-774-9)

Longing for You by Jenny Frame. When Debrek housekeeper Katie Brekman is attacked amid a burgeoning vampire-witch war, Alexis Villiers must go against everything her clan believes in to save her. (978-1-63555-658-2)

Money Creek by Anne Laughlin. Clare Lehane is a troubled lawyer from Chicago who tries to make her way in a rural town full of secrets and deceptions. (978-1-63555-795-4)

Passion's Sweet Surrender by Ronica Black. Cam and Blake are unable to deny their passion for each other, but surrendering to love is a whole different matter. (978-1-63555-703-9)

The Holiday Detour by Jane Kolven. It will take everything going wrong to make Dana and Charlie see how right they are for each other. (978-1-63555-720-6)

Too Hot to Ride by Andrews & Austin. World famous cutting horse champion and industry legend Jane Barrow is knockdown sexy in the way she moves, talks, and rides, and Rae Starr is determined not to get involved with this womanizing gambler. (978-1-63555-776-3)

A Love that Leads to Home by Ronica Black. For Carla Sims and Janice Carpenter, home isn't about location, it's where your heart is. (978-1-63555-675-9)

Blades of Bluegrass by D. Jackson Leigh. A US Army occupational therapist must rehab a bitter veteran who is a ticking political time bomb the military is desperate to disarm. (978-1-63555-637-7)

Guarding Hearts by Jaycie Morrison. As treachery and temptation threaten the women of the Women's Army Corps, who will risk it all for love? (978-1-63555-806-7)

Hopeless Romantic by Georgia Beers. Can a jaded wedding planner and an optimistic divorce attorney possibly find a future together? (978-1-63555-650-6)

Hopes and Dreams by PJ Trebelhorn. Movie theater manager Riley Warren is forced to face her high school crush and tormentor, wealthy socialite Victoria Thayer, at their twentieth reunion. (978-1-63555-670-4)

In the Cards by Kimberly Cooper Griffin. Daria and Phaedra are about to discover that love finds a way, especially when powers outside their control are at play. (978-1-63555-717-6)

Moon Fever by Ileandra Young. SPEAR agent Danika Karson must clear her werewolf friend of multiple false charges while teaching her vampire girlfriend to resist the blood mania brought on by a full moon. (978-1-63555-603-2)

Quake City by St John Karp. Can Andre find his best friend Amy before the night devolves into a nightmare of broken hearts, malevolent drag queens, and spontaneous human combustion? Or has it always happened this way, every night, at Aunty Bob's Quake City Club? (978-1-63555-723-7)

Serenity by Jesse J. Thoma. For Kit Marsden, there are many things in life she cannot change. Serenity is in the acceptance. (978-1-63555-713-8)

Sylver and Gold by Michelle Larkin. Working feverishly to find a killer before he strikes again, Boston Homicide Detective Reid Sylver and rookie cop London Gold are blindsided by their chemistry and developing attraction. (978-1-63555-611-7)

Trade Secrets by Kathleen Knowles. In Silicon Valley, love and business are a volatile mix for clinical lab scientist Tony Leung and venture capitalist Sheila Graham. (978-1-63555-642-1)

Death Overdue by David S. Pederson. Did Heath turn to murder in an alcohol induced haze to solve the problem of his blackmailer, or was it someone else who brought about a death overdue? (978-1-63555-711-4)

Entangled by Melissa Brayden. Becca Crawford is the perfect person to head up the Jade Hotel, if only the captivating owner of the local vineyard would get on board with her plan and stop badmouthing the hotel to everyone in town. (978-1-63555-709-1)

First Do No Harm by Emily Smith. Pierce and Cassidy are about to discover that when it comes to love, sometimes you have to risk it all to have it all. (978-1-63555-699-5)

Kiss Me Every Day by Dena Blake. For Wynn Evans, wishing for a do-over with Carly Jamison was a long shot, actually getting one was a game changer. (978-1-63555-551-6)

Olivia by Genevieve McCluer. In this lesbian Shakespeare adaptation with vampires, Olivia is a centuries old vampire who must fight a strange figure from her past if she wants a chance at happiness. (978-1-63555-701-5)

One Woman's Treasure by Jean Copeland. Daphne's search for discarded antiques and treasures leads to an embarrassing misunderstanding, and ultimately, the opportunity for the romance of a lifetime with Nina. (978-1-63555-652-0)

Silver Ravens by Jane Fletcher. Lori has lost her girlfriend, her home, and her job. Things don't improve when she's kidnapped and taken to fairyland. (978-1-63555-631-5)

Still Not Over You by Jenny Frame, Carsen Taite, Ali Vali. Old flames die hard in these tales of a second chance at love with the ex you're still not over. Stories by award winning authors Jenny Frame, Carsen Taite, and Ali Vali. (978-1-63555-516-5)

Storm Lines by Jessica L. Webb. Devon is a psychologist who likes rules. Marley is a cop who doesn't. They don't always agree, but both fight to protect a girl immersed in a street drug ring. (978-1-63555-626-1)

The Politics of Love by Jen Jensen. Is it possible to love across the political divide in a hostile world? Conservative Shelley Whitmore and liberal Rand Thomas are about to find out. (978-1-63555-693-3)

All the Paths to You by Morgan Lee Miller. High school sweethearts Quinn Hughes and Kennedy Reed reconnect five years after they break up and realize that their chemistry is all but over. (978-1-63555-662-9)

Arrested Pleasures by Nanisi Barrett D'Arnuck. When charged with a crime she didn't commit, Katherine Lowe faces the question: Which is harder, going to prison or falling in love? (978-1-63555-684-1)

Bonded Love by Renee Roman. Carpenter Blaze Carter suffers an injury that shatters her dreams, and ER nurse Trinity Greene hopes to show her that sometimes love is worth fighting for. (978-1-63555-530-1)

Convergence by Jane C. Esther. With life as they know it on the line, can Aerin McLeary and Olivia Ando's love survive an otherworldly threat to humankind? (978-1-63555-488-5)

Coyote Blues by Karen F. Williams. Riley Dawson, psychotherapist and shape-shifter, has her world turned upside down when Fiona Bell, her one true love, returns. (978-1-63555-558-5)

Drawn by Carsen Taite. Will the clues lead Detective Claire Hanlon to the killer terrorizing Dallas, or will she merely lose her heart to person of interest, urban artist Riley Flynn? (978-1-63555-644-5)

Every Summer Day by Lee Patton. Meant to celebrate every summer day, Luke's journal instead chronicles a love affair as fast-moving and possibly as fatal as his brother's brain tumor. (978-1-63555-706-0)

Lucky by Kris Bryant. Was Serena Evans's luck really about winning the lottery, or is she about to get even luckier in love? (978-1-63555-510-3)

The Last Days of Autumn by Donna K. Ford. Autumn and Caroline question the fairness of life, the cruelty of loss, and what it means to love as they navigate the complicated minefield of relationships, grief, and life-altering illness. (978-1-63555-672-8)

Three Alarm Response by Erin Dutton. In the midst of tragedy, can these first responders find love and healing? Three stories of courage, bravery, and passion. (978-1-63555-592-9)

Veterinary Partner by Nancy Wheelton. Callie and Lauren are determined to keep their hearts safe but find that taking a chance on love is the safest option of all. (978-1-63555-666-7)